In this exciting new duet by

**Scarlet Wilson**

discover these

**Tycoons in a Million**

*Romance in a rich man's world...*

Friends Reuben Tyler and Caleb Connor
have chosen very different paths in life.
Caleb married his sweetheart while Reuben
played the field, but they both climbed to
the dizzying heights of success!

Now, with the world at their fingertips, these
millionaires can have anything they want.
But when it comes to love, Reuben and Caleb
realize there are some things money can't buy...

The Connors' nanny, Lara Callaway,
is a breath of fresh air for rebellious Reuben
in

*Holiday with the Millionaire*

And can the Connors save their seemingly perfect
marriage?

Find out in Caleb and Addison's story...

*A Baby to Save Their Marriage*

**Available now!**

10/17

Dear Reader,

This is my second story in a duo about two friends, Reuben Tyler and Caleb Connor. Caleb and Addison Connor have the perfect life, the perfect house, the perfect son and the perfect marriage. Or do they?

For the past two years their marriage has slowly but surely been slipping away from them. They have the age-old problem of busy working lives and trying to keep up appearances, and have forgotten how to communicate with each other.

When Addison gets some earth-shattering news, the first person she should share her worries with should be her husband. But she doesn't—because she isn't sure how he will react. When Caleb tries to back out of a family holiday and gets an unexpected ultimatum from his wife, he realizes just how far they've both let things slip.

He loves his wife and his son. It's time to try to recapture what they used to have, and where better to do that than the perfect setting of Bora-Bora?

There are some serious issues in this book around prenatal screening and testing. I'm a huge supporter of screening programs but think that we often don't acknowledge how much stress a screening test can actually cause.

Happy reading!

*Scarlet Wilson*

PS: I love to hear from readers. Contact me via my website, scarlet-wilson.com.

# A Baby to Save Their Marriage

—

## Scarlet Wilson

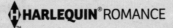

HARLEQUIN® ROMANCE

ISBN-13: 978-0-373-74389-6

A Baby to Save Their Marriage

First North American Publication 2016

Copyright © 2016 by Scarlet Wilson

**Printed in U.S.A.**

HARLEQUIN®
www.Harlequin.com

**Scarlet Wilson** writes for both Harlequin Romance and Harlequin Medical Romance. She lives on the west coast of Scotland with her fiancé and their two sons. She loves to hear from readers and can be reached via her website, scarlet-wilson.com.

This book is dedicated to my two honorary "crazy" nieces, Sarah Mason and Jakki Lee. Just remember in later life I'll blackmail you with all the stories!

# CHAPTER ONE

ADDISON WAS PACING. She couldn't help it. It was three o'clock and Caleb still wasn't home. They had to leave for the airport in an hour and he hadn't even packed.

The doorbell rang and she hurried to answer. Lara, her son Tristan's nanny, stood on the doorstep, rain dripping from her hair and nose.

'Lara? What on earth? Come in, come in.'

Lara stumbled over the doorstep, dragging a large suitcase behind her. 'I'm so sorry, Addison. I know you're just about to leave for your holiday. But I had nowhere else to go.'

'What's wrong?' Addison was trying not to panic. Lara was the perfect nanny. Her son Tristan adored her. It didn't matter they were about to go on a month-long holiday, she wanted to be sure Lara wasn't in any kind of trouble.

Lara sniffed. 'I had a *Sliding* Doors moment. I got the earlier Tube home and Josh…' her voice wobbled '…he was in bed with the next-door neighbour.' Her shoulders started to shake.

'What? He what?' Addison was enraged. 'That lazy, good-for-nothing ratbag. You've paid the rent for how long? He doesn't even contribute and he treats you like that?' She'd never liked Lara's boyfriend and now she knew exactly why.

She put her arm around Lara's shoulders and guided her into the kitchen, pressing a few buttons on her coffee machine.

'Here, let me get you something.' The machine only took a few minutes, then she sat down across from Lara. 'What are you going to do?'

Lara bit her lip. 'I'm sorry, I panicked. I just stuffed a case and left. I know this is the last thing you need right now.'

Addison silently sucked in a breath. Lara was perceptive. Addison had never said a word to her but she'd obviously picked up on the stress in the household.

'What do you need?'

Lara seemed nervous. 'I was wondering… I'll need to find somewhere else to stay. Is there any chance I could stay here while you're away?'

Something simple. 'Absolutely. No problem at all.' She stood up. 'And, Lara? Don't give up your holiday. You saved long and hard for that.

Don't let him spoil it for you. Go, and enjoy every second without him.' She reached over and gave Lara's shoulder a squeeze. 'Now, will you be okay? Caleb and I will be out of your hair within the hour. I need to finish packing.'

Lara gave a nod and a grateful smile. 'Thanks, Addison. I owe you, big time.'

Addison met her gaze. 'You deserve someone who loves and respects you, just remember that.'

She walked out of the kitchen and into the large hallway just as the door opened again. Caleb. Also soaked to the skin and still on his phone.

She felt herself prickle. 'Caleb? Do you know—?'

He gestured to her to stop talking as he continued his conversation. 'Frank, I know exactly how important this is. I will deal with it. I promise you. The price of the stock won't fall. I've been working on these negotiations for months. I'm not about to let anything get in the way.'

He looked tired. His shirt and trousers were wrinkled and she knew that he'd worked through the night. He was doing that more and more now as the business had just exploded.

With Caleb, she would never need to worry about another woman. He didn't have enough hours in the day for her and Tristan, let alone another woman. For the last three years his work had been everything. They'd drifted further and further apart. The man she used to love cuddling up to barely came to bed any more. If he wasn't working at his office in the city, he was working in his office in the house.

Her work had exploded too. She'd started as a naïve young student who'd lost her sister to ovarian cancer, setting up a website and trying to get information out to others. Then, a famous celebrity had been diagnosed with the same cancer—and credited the information she'd read on Addison's site as being the catalyst for her challenging her doctor's diagnosis. After that, things had just gone crazy.

The last ten years had been a whirlwind. She'd met Caleb at a charity auction and fallen head over heels in love. They'd got married, had Tristan and life had seemed perfect. She'd hired some people to help her with the charity and Caleb's business had started to take off.

To the outside world they were the perfect couple—the perfect family. She couldn't deny her husband was handsome; even with the deep furrows in his brow and tired lines around his eyes he could still make her heart flutter. Tristan, their son, was like a mini-me version of his father. They lived in one of the best areas in London.

But a few weeks ago she'd got a wake-up call.

Something she hadn't even had a chance to sit down and talk to her husband about.

That was when she'd realised just how far they'd slipped from one another. That was when she'd booked this holiday and told Caleb to arrange the time off. She had some major decisions to make. And they desperately needed some time away together as a family. She needed to be able to talk to her husband without fear of a phone ringing or an email pinging into his inbox to distract him.

He was still talking into his mobile. He'd barely even acknowledged her. Her stomach gave a little twist. She couldn't keep living like this. This wasn't living. It was existing.

This was the man who'd made her laugh, cry and scream with excitement when they'd first met. This was the man who'd spent every single night taking her in his arms and talking until the early hours of the morning. Then, he'd get up early and bring her breakfast in bed. When they'd got married he'd surprised her by flying in her friends from all over the world—all expenses covered. When she'd shown him the pregnancy test one morning he'd whooped with joy and by the time she'd got home after work the house had been filled with pink and blue helium balloons.

A million special memories of a relationship that seemed to have died.

A few weeks ago she'd tried to arrange something special. Lara had watched Tristan and she'd spent hours preparing Caleb's favourite meal, setting the table and lighting candles on their rarely used dining table. She'd changed into a dark pink dress that he'd bought her a few years earlier and sat and waited for him to appear. And waited…and waited…and waited.

The silver dome covering the second pregnancy test had never been lifted.

The candles had finally burned down and gone out. The dinner had been ruined and her dress tossed back into the wardrobe. He hadn't got in until just after two a.m.—that was when she'd finally felt the sag of the bed as he'd sat down.

She'd never mentioned a thing to him. A tiny little part of her was worried. They'd disagreed a year earlier about expanding their family. She'd been keen—but Caleb hadn't.

She'd been hoping and praying that he'd be delighted they were unexpectedly pregnant—just as he'd been the last time. And that tiny little seed of doubt had allowed itself to take root and grow over the last few weeks because it just felt as if he was slipping further and further away from her.

The phone rang and she picked it up. Caleb was still talking on his mobile—still not even looking at her.

'Hello, can I speak to Addison Connor please?'

She vaguely recognised the voice. 'This is Mrs Connor.'

'Ah, Addison. It's Dr Mackay.'

It was like a cool breeze dancing over her skin. Her obstetrician. She'd seen him last week to have her pregnancy confirmed and her first scan and tests.

Her eyes went automatically to Caleb. She was conscious he would be able to hear her words but he was far too engrossed in his own phone call to notice her.

'What can I do for you?'

The doctor hesitated. 'I wonder if you would be able to come along to the clinic later today, or tomorrow.'

The cool breeze turned into an arctic chill. 'Why?'

'We need to have a chat.'

'I'm leaving in an hour's time. I'll be out of the country for a month. I can't come to the clinic. If you need to discuss something with me then do it now.'

She was being curt. But she couldn't help it. This didn't sound like good news. Everything had seemed fine the other day. Her ultrasound had appeared fine and her pregnancy had seemed to be progressing as normal.

She heard him draw in a deep breath. 'This isn't ideal. I'd prefer to do this face to face.'

'I'm sorry, that just isn't possible. What do you need to tell me?'

He gave a sigh. 'We need to talk about your test results from your NT test.'

She straightened up. 'The measurement at the back of neck? I saw that being done. The...' She glanced towards Caleb. She'd almost said sonographer. But he'd turned his back and was facing into their front room. 'The technician never said there was a problem.' She paid attention. She could remember the sonographer taking a few minutes to take the tiny measurement needed.

'I realise that. But you'll know that we calculate risk based on a number of things. We use the nuchal translucency measurement, along with the blood test and mother's age, to calculate risk. Our tests at this stage show you could be at higher risk of having a baby affected by Down's syndrome.'

Her heart skipped a beat. 'How high?'

All other noise just faded into the background. The only thing she could focus on right now was what the doctor was saying.

He spoke clearly. 'The screening test gives

us a range. We would normally expect the measurement of a nuchal translucency test to be under three point five millimetres. Yours was slightly above that at three point seven. A woman of thirty would normally have a risk of around one in a thousand. Along with your age and your blood test results it means that your risk of having a baby affected by Down's syndrome is around one in one hundred and forty.'

There was a roaring sound in her ears. This wasn't happening. This couldn't be happening. Everything had looked fine. She'd had this test before when she was pregnant with Tristan. No one had phoned her then. She'd just received a letter in the post a week later saying she was low risk.

'Mrs Connor?'

'I thought you were more at risk if you were in your forties. I've just turned thirty.' Her brain was trying to make sense of what she'd just been told.

'Age can be a factor, but that's not always the case. If you'd like we can consider some other tests. You've just passed the first trimester of pregnancy so we're too late for a CVS test.'

She had no idea what he was talking about.

'But we could arrange an amniocentesis at fifteen weeks. Along with other detailed scans.'

'That has risks, doesn't it?'

'There is a small risk of miscarriage associated with amniocentesis.'

'Then, no. In fact, no to other tests. I don't want any. It won't change my mind about anything.'

There was a few seconds' silence. From the other side of the room Caleb caught her eye momentarily. A few years ago he'd been her rock—her everything. But as she was hearing this news today she'd never felt so alone.

'Mrs Connor, I'll support you in any decision. You would be offered a detailed scan routinely at twenty weeks. I'd really like you to still attend. If your child is affected by Down's syndrome there is a chance of cardiac defects. It's something we could pick up on the scan and plan for prior to your delivery. It's really in the best interests of your child.'

She tried to be rational. She took a deep breath and paused a few seconds to think. She could remember having the detailed scan with Tristan. That was when they'd found out they were having a little boy. They'd been so excited as soon as they'd left the scan room they'd headed to the nearest baby shop to look for baby-boy clothes.

She squeezed her eyes closed for a few seconds. Now, she felt as if she couldn't even rely on Caleb to make time in his diary for their baby scan. In her head she could already see herself attending alone.

The background noise that had muted before became crystal clear.

Caleb was still on the phone. 'I can do that tonight. No problem. Just give me a bit of time.' He glanced over towards Addison and jerked when he saw her watching him. 'There's something I need to sort out at home.'

Anger sparked through her. Was he talking about her? Had he forgotten they were supposed to be leaving for the airport in less than an hour?

Her stomach turned over. Oh, no. He wouldn't dare? Would he?

She turned her attention back to the phone. 'Of course I'll attend. I leave today and will be gone for a month. Can I make an appointment to see you when I come back?'

'Of course, Mrs Connor. My secretary will arrange that and get both appointments to you shortly. In the meantime, if you need to contact me, please feel free.'

Addison put down the phone and turned to face Caleb.

He took a step towards her. 'Addison—honey…'

When was the last time he'd called her that? Was it when he'd missed Tristan singing Christmas carols at nursery? Or was it when he'd promised to bath Tristan and put him to bed but got delayed at work once again? Tristan had finally fallen asleep clutching the book he'd wanted Caleb to read to him.

She held up her hand. 'Get packed, Caleb. Taxi will be here in forty minutes.'

He held up his phone. 'Things have gone crazy at work. This merger is just huge. It's taking up every hour of every day. Timing is crucial. I just can't go away right now. As for four weeks? It's just far too long. There's no way I can make that work. I have to be here.'

All the pent-up rage, frustration and disappointment that had been bubbling under the surface for the last three years erupted to the surface.

'Everything takes up every hour of the day for you, Caleb—or haven't you noticed? You don't even seem to realise you have a family any more. You're never here and when you are here, you might as well not be.'

He flinched. But she wasn't sorry. She'd had too many let-downs over the last year and too many dinners for one to care any more.

He shook his head. 'That's not fair, Addison.'

'That's not fair? That's not fair?' She couldn't help it. She was shouting now. 'Let me tell you what's not fair. Your son, spending the whole time at nursery with his eyes fixed on the door when he was singing his Christmas carols and waiting for you to appear. I know you said there was an emergency at work—something that couldn't wait—but try explaining that to a four-year-old.' She pointed to herself. 'It's not you that has to see his face, Caleb. It's me.'

She could see the pure frustration on his face. He dropped his case and ran his fingers through his still-damp hair. He could barely meet her gaze. And that just made her worse.

'Please stop.'

She was shaking now. This had been building for a while. They'd needed to sit down and talk for a long time. But they just hadn't got around to it—probably because Caleb was never there.

It was a miracle she was pregnant at all. But twelve weeks ago had been the last time they'd made love after Caleb had fallen into bed late one night. She'd had the faintest glimmer of hope that maybe he'd start noticing her again, maybe he'd start talking. It had been their anniversary and she'd thought that he'd forgotten. For their first few anniversaries they'd always made a fuss of each other and gone away to a hotel overnight. He'd finally come home clutching a beautiful bunch of flowers, a hastily written card and a thin gold bracelet that came from a jeweller's based inside a popular London hotel—it was probably the only place that was open late at night. The effort had brought tears to her eyes and ignited a spark of passion that had been missing between them for a while. She'd hoped that it would be a turning point for them both. But the next day had been no different from all the others.

'This deal is crucial. I've been working on it for months. The next couple of weeks will be the most vital. I *need* to be here.'

'You *need* to be with your family.'

He held up his hands. 'Maybe I could come out in a few weeks, once things have quietened down, and spend some time with you and Tristan then?'

'But things never quieten down. You and I both know that, Caleb.' She straightened her shoulders. She'd had enough. She'd been pushed as far as she could go and tolerated as much as she could.

This was the point of no return.

'In thirty minutes' time, Tristan and I are leaving for the airport. If you're not on that plane with us, when we come back in a month, we won't be coming back here.'

'What?' His eyes widened.

'I'm done, Caleb. I'm done with Tristan and I playing second best to everything else in your life. Let me make this easy for you. Make a decision. You have thirty minutes.'

Caleb Connor's life seemed to be falling apart around him. He'd never seen his beautiful wife look so angry. But there was more than that: she looked cold—something he'd never associated with Addison.

He'd come home, hoping to placate her and send her and Tristan on the holiday she'd insisted on booking. She'd seemed so unhappy recently and he knew it was partly his fault.

She was right. He was never here. Work just seemed to have taken over his whole life. He'd won an award a few years ago as Business Person of the Year and since then everything had skyrocketed.

And things just kept slipping. The nursery carol service, putting Tristan to bed, and he was sure he'd missed a few things he was supposed to be doing with Addison. But she'd never said anything. He'd just got the frosty reception when he'd come home at night. Most times he hadn't even noticed the frosty reception because he'd been so late Addison had already been sleeping.

It was a mistake. And he knew it. But right now was a vital time. He, and his partner, were building their business. Making sure they had a good foundation and reputation on which to base other business. This was a temporary situation. He'd never expected Addison to react like this. He'd never seen her act like this before.

But that wasn't all. She looked pale. She looked worried. And that was before she told him she and Tristan might not come back.

'Addison, be reasonable.'

Her voice chilled him. 'I've spent the last three years being reasonable and making excuses for you never being around. I'm done. I'm done doing that. I manage to get a work-life balance and so should you. If your family isn't your priority, then you don't deserve a family.'

The words stung. But the truth was he couldn't be completely surprised. Things had been strained for so long. What had happened to the relaxed, happy people they both used to be? Last year they'd finally employed a nanny when Addison had felt her work commitments had increased. Lara had been a blessing. But Addison still made time for Tristan. She never missed any of his doctor's appointments or nursery performances.

Not like him.

A wave of guilt washed over him.

'Maybe we could wait, maybe we could go somewhere later in the year?'

Addison picked up the notepad she'd been writing on next to the phone.

She sighed. 'Then it will be another deal, another business. I'm tired of this. Decide what your priorities are. Because I've had enough.'

'You're giving me an ultimatum?'

He couldn't believe it. It felt like a bolt out of the blue. And he couldn't believe Addison was actually behaving like this.

She walked over to him and looked up at him with her clear green eyes. He'd never seen them look so sincere. There was no hesitation. None at all. 'Yes, I am.' She turned and walked up the stairs.

He sagged against the wall as his phone rang again. He pulled it out of his pocket. Harry. His partner. He'd need to talk to him later.

He shrugged off his damp coat. What on earth was he going to do? He had a million different things still to sort out for this deal. He'd assumed he would come home, placate Addison, give both her and Tristan a kiss, send them on their way and get back to work.

'Daddy!' Tristan ran down the stairs towards him. 'Come and see what I've packed.'

His heart melted as he scooped the little guy up into his arms. Tristan kept talking. 'We're going on a big plane. And then on a little plane. Can you buy a plane, Daddy?'

He walked up the stairs towards Tristan's room. 'Daddy, you're all wet. What have you been doing?'

He smiled. 'I've been out in the rain.'

He set Tristan down at the entrance to his room and Tristan dive-bombed on top of his neatly packed case. 'Whee! Look, Daddy, I've sneaked in some extra toys.' He peered over his shoulder. 'Shh…don't tell Mummy.'

Caleb sat down on the bed and glanced in the case. Sure enough, tucked in between socks and suncream were a whole array of wrestlers and a tiny army of cars. He let out a laugh. Tristan always did this. Addison would tell him he was allowed to bring two wrestlers, or two cars, depending on where they were going, and Tristan would find a way to sneak another few into his pockets, Addison's bag or, on occasion, Caleb's briefcase.

He felt a little pang. When was the last time Tristan had done that?

And more importantly, why would it be his briefcase? It felt as if it were permanently attached to his hand—and that must be the way it seemed to his son.

He leaned forward as he watched Tristan play. A full-blown wrestling match had started above the clothes. When was the last time he'd watched Tristan play?

Everything Addison had just said to him was firing off sparks in his brain. In most instances, he was searching desperately for memories of the last time he'd done something with his wife and son. And the more he searched, the guiltier he felt.

She'd meant it. She'd looked into his eyes and meant it when she'd said they wouldn't come home.

He'd thought Addison and he would be together for ever. At least, that was what it used to feel like. He'd already decided a few days ago that there was no way he could go on this holiday. He just actually hadn't taken the time to sit down and talk to his wife about it.

More fool him.

Something was wrong. Something was very wrong and he hadn't paid attention until around ten minutes ago.

He knew exactly what had happened to Addison.

*He had.*

He pulled his phone out of his pocket as he watched Tristan. He was still in charge of the wrestling match. He was so happy and good-natured. He couldn't ask for a better son.

Tristan glanced at him and thrust a wrestler towards him. 'Here, Daddy, you can have this one. He's getting old, like you.'

There was such an innocence in his words. Tristan thought he was old? But of course he did. He'd spent the last three years looking tired and that would be all the memories that Tristan had of him.

He looked around the room. It was still decorated in baby blues. Underneath the bed was a pile of fresh wallpaper, bedding and stickers all covered in pictures of planets. He'd promised to decorate around eight months ago. The pile had been there ever since.

But there was more. Addison had brought up the subject of having another baby around a year ago.

He'd always imagined they'd have a big family. He'd always wanted to have a big family.

But her words had gripped him in a way he hadn't expected.

They'd never really sat down and discussed it. But Addison had paled into a shadow of herself in the months after giving birth to Tristan. He'd helped as much as he could. He'd frequently got up and done the night feeds. He'd made excuses for not being at work. He'd stayed around as frequently as he could, at first, to try and give her a break, and then to try and get them to spend time together as a family. For the first few months her face had been almost blank when she'd looked at Tristan. It had felt as if she were slipping away a little more each day.

He'd spoken to the GP. He'd spoken to the health visitor—asking what else he could do. They'd reassured him he was doing everything he could and just to be patient. Finally, he'd seen little glimpses of his wife again. A smile when she saw Tristan smile. A willingness to take part. The dark circles had eventually dimmed beneath her eyes and the spark of life that always surrounded her had finally emerged again.

He couldn't let that happen to her again. *He* wouldn't do that to his wife again.

As he stared around Tristan's room it was as if everything came crashing down on him all at once.

He'd thought he might lose his family once before.

There was no way he could let this happen. There was no way he was letting his family slip through his fingers. The thought of coming home at night to an empty house filled him with horror.

He had to sort this. He had to. He didn't want to imagine his world without them in it.

He pressed the redial button on his phone. 'Harry, there's been a change of plan.'

His phone buzzed as he kept talking. He walked through to the bedroom. Addison wasn't there. A large suitcase was sitting open on the bed, completely empty. It must be for him.

As Harry kept talking Caleb reached into his large wardrobe and picked up a whole stack of T-shirts, dropping them into the suitcase exactly the way they were. He had to lean further back to find a pile of shorts. He sent a silent prayer above that they might actually still fit as he threw them and some swimming shorts into the case. Underwear was easy. He pulled out one entire drawer and tipped it up into the case.

Feet. What would he wear on his feet?

He looked down. His feet were damp from his earlier walk through the soaked London streets. He kicked off his shoes and dropped his trousers to the floor. His shirt was pulled over his head and abandoned with the rest of his things on the floor.

What to travel in? He grabbed a pair of three-quarter-length trousers and a polo shirt, sticking his feet into a pair of baseball boots and throwing some others in the case.

Tristan appeared at the door and smiled at his father's packing efforts. He tucked a few wrestlers into the case along with a London bus, New York taxi cab and space shuttle. 'I had a few spares. I'll give you a little loan.'

Caleb laughed. By the time Tristan was finished the entire contents of his room would be hidden between the three cases.

Caleb looked around. Was he done? His brief-case sat in the corner of the room. The charging cables for his phone and laptop were in there. He'd be able to work wherever they were. Internet was everywhere these days and as for international calls? He'd just need to swallow the costs.

A quick check of the en suite gave him some deodorant, his toothbrush and his shaving gear. At the last second he reached over to grab some aftershave and then stopped, put it back, and grabbed another one from under the sink. Harry had finally finished talking.

'I'll be at the airport in an hour. I'll send you that report from the lounge.' He rang off. The buzz had been a text message.

His best friend, Reuben Tyler. He was on his way back from LA. Reuben's roof had been undergoing repairs and the roofers had discovered asbestos. He couldn't stay there. He knew Caleb was going on holiday, could he stay at his?

Caleb dashed off a reply telling him where the key was and how to turn off the alarm. Best not mention it to Addison. Reuben wasn't exactly her favourite of Caleb's friends.

He glanced at the case. Done. What else

could he need? Why did some people spend days packing?

He zipped it up and picked it off the bed.

As he walked down the stairs he heard the taxi beep outside.

'Come on, Tristan!' shouted Addison. 'It's time to go.'

She hadn't noticed him yet. Was she really just going to walk out of the front door without talking to him again?

The taxi driver appeared at the door and picked up the two waiting cases.

Tristan bolted down the stairs ahead of him carrying two wrestlers. Addison smiled and shook her head. 'No way, you've already got ten in your backpack. That's the limit.' She held out his small red baseball jacket and waited for him to slide his arms inside.

She'd changed. She was wearing cream casual trousers and a pink top.

Caleb cleared his throat.

Addison did a double take. She was shocked. She was stunned that he'd actually packed and changed. Did she really think that little of him? Did she really think that he'd just let his wife and child leave without a fight?

'You've packed.'

He stepped forward and sat his case down. 'I've packed.' He looked her straight in the eye.

She blinked and picked up the passport she'd left sitting on the side table and slid it into her bag.

The taxi driver stuck his head inside and picked up the case. 'Last one?'

Caleb nodded.

'And where we headed?'

'Heathrow.'

Caleb cringed inwardly. He couldn't even remember where they were going. He knew it was hot. It might be the Caribbean, or the Seychelles—somewhere like that. He remembered her mentioning it was a long flight, first stop LA and after that…

Nope. He just couldn't remember. It hadn't registered in his brain.

Like so many other things.

He turned back to pick up his briefcase. Addison frowned and he tried not to be annoyed.

He was coming on holiday. He would be spending time with them. But he also needed to do some work. Surely she could understand that?

She took Tristan's hand firmly in hers. 'Let's go, honey, we need to get on the big plane.'

'Come on, Daddy!' yelled Tristan over his shoulder.

Caleb glanced at the abandoned wrestlers on the side table. He picked them up and tucked them in his briefcase. Anything to keep the little guy happy.

Addison was strapping Tristan into the back of the cab.

She straightened up and stretched her back. 'Okay?' he asked as he walked up behind her.

She didn't even answer the question. Her mind seemed to be away in a world of its own.

He paused before he climbed in the cab. 'Addison, everything will be fine.'

He didn't want to acknowledge what had just happened between them. He didn't want to acknowledge the fact his wife had just issued him with an ultimatum. He didn't want to give brain space to the fact she'd just threatened to leave.

Her clear green eyes met his. 'Will it?' she asked before she climbed in the cab and slammed the door, staring straight ahead.

Caleb swallowed. Addison seemed anything but fine.

Where did they go from here?

# CHAPTER TWO

THREE HOURS LATER they were finally on their flight. Addison had felt herself silently fume as Caleb had spent most of his time on his computer or on his phone in the business lounge while she kept Tristan entertained.

Her head was in turmoil. She wanted to snatch the computer from his hands and search for everything she could find on nuchal screening and being labelled high risk.

But that wouldn't help her. Nothing would help her right now. Her heart had flip-flopped when Dr Mackay had told her children with Down's syndrome could have heart problems. Somewhere in the back of her mind she'd heard that before. Weren't there other associated conditions? She just didn't know enough about these things. She had no background knowledge in anything medical related.

At some point she would need to tell Caleb

about the pregnancy. Then, she'd need to tell him about the phone call.

She wasn't sure how he would react to any of it.

She was still shocked that he'd actually come.

It was weird. Even though things had been awkward between them, if you'd asked her a few days ago, she would never have thought that Caleb would try and back out of the holiday.

Even though she'd reminded him on a few occasions to pack his case—and he hadn't got around to it—she'd still hoped he'd remember.

But when he'd been late back today and been so busy on his phone her heart had sunk like a stone. And when he'd actually started to say that he was too busy and the timing didn't suit she'd wanted to throw something at him.

That had been it. That had been the point that the mist had come down and she'd been at the point of no return. The phone call hadn't helped. But it hadn't been the catalyst. Caleb and his complete disregard of her and Tristan had been the catalyst.

When she'd given him the ultimatum she'd actually thought he wouldn't come. She'd actually thought she'd just called time on their marriage.

She'd had to disappear into one of the empty

bathrooms upstairs to allow herself some silent sobs.

All she could think about right now was how she would cope on her own with two children. Tristan was just a ball of energy. He would be over the moon to find out he was going to have a little brother or sister. But Tristan had been a poor sleeper. He'd suffered from colic and no amount of remedies or different kinds of bottles had helped. Sometimes at night he'd screamed for hours. She'd only managed to cope because she'd had Caleb right by her side.

He'd always known when to send her back to bed and disappear with the screaming Tristan downstairs. A few hours later she'd find him slumped on the sofa with a peaceful Tristan sleeping on his chest.

How would she manage if this baby was the same and there was no Caleb to help?

She sucked in a deep breath. She'd never felt so unsettled. She'd never felt so restless. She'd never felt so alone.

She was scared. The next few weeks would tell her everything she needed to know. Whether she was in this alone, or whether her husband would be at her side.

They couldn't keep going the way they were. Somewhere along the line they'd lost each other.

'Flight 234 to LAX is now boarding at Gate Twelve.'

She sat upright. 'Come on, Tristan, that's us. It's time to go.'

He scrambled to his feet, anxious to get on board the plane. Caleb was still typing away on his computer.

Addison couldn't help a silent smirk. When he reached their destination he'd get a huge wake-up call when he realised there was no phone line and no Internet. Did he honestly think it was acceptable to come on holiday with his family and spend his time working?

Sometimes Caleb had rocks in his head.

She boarded the plane with Tristan and helped him set up his television for a kids' show. She didn't say a word when Caleb finally sat down next to them.

The stewardess appeared. 'Champagne?'

'Apple juice, please.'

Caleb looked surprised but didn't comment. He accepted the glass of champagne and started sipping.

The ten-hour flight took them well into the middle of the night and Tristan spent a good part of it fast asleep. When they had to change planes at LAX for Tahiti, Caleb carried him through the airport and settled him back into his seat on the next plane.

Eight hours later they switched onto their final fifty-minute flight to the Bora Boras.

As they'd landed in Tahiti his phone had beeped. He'd pulled it out of his pocket, glanced at it and pushed it away again.

She felt a little twinge. Maybe she should warn him that after the next flight he wouldn't get a signal? But part of her was afraid he might refuse to get on the next plane. And she was just too exhausted to have another fight.

She hadn't been able to relax on any of the flights so far. She was too keyed up. Her mind was constantly spinning. By the time she reached the Bora Boras she would be fit only to fall into bed.

The small white plane had only fifty passengers. Even though she was absolutely exhausted, the view from the plane was spectacular. The travel agent had told her that writers and artists called the Bora Boras the most beautiful islands in the world. They weren't wrong.

For this part of the journey, she was glad she was still awake.

The aerial view of the green, jagged volcanic peak of towering Mount Otemanu appeared on the horizon. It was surrounded by a captivating, vivid blue lagoon. As they descended she was amazed by the many blues of the Bora Bora lagoon. It wasn't one island, instead it was a collection. The airport was on its own islet, one of a number of small barrier islands forming a ring around the lagoon. There were a variety of resorts set on the beautiful sandy beaches. Some extended out over the lagoon with their wooden walkways connecting to thatched-roof overwater bungalows. Others had lodges perched on the steep hillside and some had hideaway villas set right on the water's edge. Each resort seemed more beautiful than the one before.

Fifty minutes later they had arrived in paradise.

'Welcome to the Bora Boras,' shouted the pilot as they landed.

The airport was small. A smart dark-skinned man was waiting with a sign saying Connor.

He gave them a polite nod and took their luggage, guiding them over to a glistening white boat on a wooden pier. Caleb stopped and looked around. The view of the blue lagoon was dazzling, bright turquoise next to white sandy beaches. And even though the lagoon was a hive of activity, it also had an air of tranquillity about it.

'Wow,' he said quietly.

Addison pressed her lips together. This was entirely what she'd wanted to capture. A bit of peace. A bit of luxury. And a bit of togetherness. Would they really be able to capture all three?

'We get to go on a boat!' shouted Tristan. She'd no idea where he got his energy from. After twenty hours of travel she'd expected him to be as exhausted as she was. But he'd slept part way on both flights while, no matter how hard she tried, she just couldn't sleep sitting up.

They climbed on board the sleek white boat. Tristan ran up to the front where he could watch the boat being steered. It didn't take long to cross the beautiful lagoon and drop them at their resort where they were met with staff greeting them with fresh leis, who picked up their bags and checked them in. Their bungalow sat on the white sandy beach. It had a large sitting room and kitchen, with two bedrooms and a master suite that opened out onto the beach. The rooms were luxurious while still paying homage to the Polynesian style. They also had a small over-water bungalow with thatched roof and walkway and its own hot tub. Tristan couldn't hide his excitement when he saw the glass panel in the floor with fish swimming underneath in the tropical waters. 'Look, Mummy, look!'

It couldn't be more perfect. She'd been nervous about them staying in the bungalows over water since Tristan was coming with them. But this had been a compromise. This way she had the safety of a beach house with the magic of the water bungalow too.

She unpacked their clothes as Caleb looked around. The first thing he unpacked was his computer. Apart from when stepping off the plane, he hadn't really taken in the beauty around them.

She tried to hide her frustration but twenty hours of travel would wear anyone's patience thin.

She dug out Tristan's beach wear and covered him in suncream. It took him less than a minute to run across the sand and start digging with his spade and splashing in the water. She changed into her swimming costume and arranged herself under the nearby parasol and sun lounger where she could watch him.

Her peace lasted less than five minutes.

'How do I connect to the Internet?' Caleb asked from the doorway of the bungalow.

'You don't.'

He frowned. 'What do you mean?'

She shook her head. 'There is no Internet.'

The furrows on his brow deepened. He hadn't changed his clothes or stopped to appreciate their surroundings. 'There has to be. Where is the phone line?'

She shrugged. 'I don't think there is one. There's an intercom that links to Reception if we need anything. I think we just use that.'

She was doing her absolute best to appear casual. It was pretty ironic really since she was staring over at the volcanic peak of Mount Otemanu. She absolutely knew that when he realised there was definitely no phone or Internet he'd go off with more explosions than Mount Otemanu ever had.

The doors to the house were wide open so she could hear him moving around inside. Part of her felt a little sad. They'd just landed in paradise and he hadn't come out to play with his son in the sand, or to sit next to her on the sun lounger. It made her absolutely determined that she'd made the right decision. She needed a chance to see her husband again. She needed a chance to see how he was without any of the trappings of work attached to him. *They* needed a chance to be stripped bare. And this was the only place to do it. There was no room for distractions here. It was just them, and Tristan.

And the secret baby package.

She looked back at the bungalow and watched as he paced around inside, stressing and searching the room for any hidden phone lines or Wi-Fi connections.

The Caleb Connor that she'd met ten years ago would never have stressed about being constantly connected to the world. He would never have spent time on holiday virtually ignoring his wife and child.

This was the life she led now. And this was the reason she knew she had to take a step to see if this marriage could be saved. She would never introduce another child into this way of life.

Oh, no matter what the outcome of this holiday, she would always have this baby. But she wanted to be prepared. She wanted to have time to plan, to know whether she would be doing this alone or not—particularly if she and her baby needed additional support.

One in one hundred and forty. Most people would think the odds were in their favour.

In one hundred and thirty-nine chances the baby wouldn't be affected.

But in one of those chances it would.

She'd thought about this before. When she'd had Tristan she'd been told she was low risk. But her midwife had carefully explained that low risk didn't equal *no* risk. There was always that possibility. And she'd understood that then, just as she did now.

It was amazing how much this had caused her to focus. The holiday had been booked. Since she'd found out she was pregnant she knew she needed to deal with the elephant in the room. In fact, she was pretty sure an elephant could have been sitting in their front room and Caleb wouldn't have noticed. That was how distant he'd been.

The distance made her uncomfortable. It reminded her of a time before—a time that seemed a little hazy for her—a time where the distance between them had been her fault. She squeezed her eyes closed for a second. She didn't like to remember anything about that.

She heard a loud beep. It was Caleb on the intercom. 'How do I connect to the Internet?'

The bright sing-song voice answered straight away. 'No Internet here. Sorry.'

'What do you mean there's no Internet? Everywhere has Internet. There must be somewhere I can get a connection?' She could hear the anger in his voice. It drifted out of the doors towards them and Tristan, who had come back to play next to her, looked up from digging in the sand. She shook her head and he put his head back down and kept building his castle.

'No connection on the Bora Boras, sir.'

'What about a phone? Can I have access to a phone?'

'Only radio contact with the mainland, sir. That's the beauty of our resort. Most people come here specially.'

She heard the click again then the thudding footsteps. A few seconds later the small amount of sun sneaking under the parasol was blocked out.

He had his hands on his hips. His lips were

pressed tightly together and there was a tic in his jaw. 'Tell me you know where the Wi-Fi is.' There was a tad of desperation in his voice.

She pushed her sunglasses up on her head and pressed her hand against her chest in mock horror. 'There's no Wi-Fi?' She sagged back against the sun lounger. 'Tragedy.' She shot him a little smile. 'Your computer and phone will probably spontaneously combust now. Just as well there's a perfect ocean to throw them in.'

He sighed and sat down, running his fingers through his hair. 'Oh, Addison. I'm in the middle of a deal right now. This could make or break our company. The only reason I came was because I knew I could still work remotely.'

'And that's why I didn't tell you.'

She put her hand on Tristan's shoulder. 'Why don't you go inside and have a little lie down for a while? I'll come inside and put a DVD on for you.' He disappeared quickly into the bungalow.

Addison swung her legs around and stood up, the warm sand beneath her feet.

'You're absolutely right. I deliberately picked a place with no phone and no Internet. Ask yourself why. You've forgotten we even exist. You treat us as if we're not important. This deal could make or break your company?' She waved her hand. 'I've heard that for the last three years.

Maybe the first time I believed it. But every time after that? I don't think so.'

She stepped closer to him. Close enough that she could see the exhaustion in his face and the fine lines that had appeared all around his eyes. 'What I do believe is that the only reason you came is because you thought you could work here remotely.' She shook her head. 'Think about that for a minute, Caleb. Just think about it. Do you think that's normal for a family holiday? Do you think that's what most husbands and fathers do on holiday?'

He at least had the good sense to look embarrassed. 'You know how important this is.'

'No, Caleb. I know how important you *think* it is. There's a difference. I think you'll find that in the scale of life it's not that important at all.'

Now he looked annoyed again. 'Well, in order to pay the mortgage and the bills I think you'll find work is important.'

'More important than your family?'

He waved his hand. 'Now you're just being ridiculous.'

'No. No, I'm not. And don't worry about your business. Harry will deal with everything. He's more than capable.'

'And how do you know that?'

She sighed. 'Because I spoke to him before

we left. He knew that once you got here you'd have no phone, no Internet.'

Caleb looked stunned. 'What? Harry knew?'

She started to walk away. She'd had enough of this. 'Of course he knew. Seems like he didn't think it was such a bad idea. And you can stop checking your phone for emails or messages. There are no signal towers out here. I'm actually surprised Harry messaged you at all.'

Caleb shook his head. 'Earlier? In Tahiti? It wasn't Harry. It was Reuben.'

She couldn't help it. She raised her eyebrows. She always did that when she heard this name. 'Reuben Tyler? What did he want?'

Caleb shrugged. 'He needed somewhere to stay. His flat's got asbestos in the roof. I told him he could stay at ours.'

Her mouth fell open. 'You did what?'

He seemed surprised. 'What's the big deal? We're not there. The house is empty.'

'Oh, no.' Now she started pacing. 'The house isn't empty. Lara. Lara's in the house.'

Now Caleb looked confused. 'Why would Lara be in the house? I never saw her.'

Addison spun around. 'She appeared just before you did. Seems she went home and found her boyfriend in bed with the neighbour.' She threw up her hands. 'This is what I'm talking about, Caleb. She was right there. Right there sitting in our kitchen. You didn't even notice.'

He frowned. 'Reuben will be expecting the place to be empty. That's what I told him.'

'And Lara will be expecting to have the house to herself. She needs a bit of time to sort herself out. The last thing she needs right now is Reuben Tyler. She won't even know who he is.'

Caleb shook his head. 'Well, it's too late now. They'll both be in the house and according to you we have no way to get in touch.'

Addison cringed. He was right. There was no way to get in touch. The world seemed to love Reuben Tyler but she didn't. Probably because she'd walked in one night just as he'd taken a swing at her husband. Caleb had said it was nothing. But it wasn't nothing to her.

'There's really no Internet?'

'We're back to that again?'

He nodded. She could see the stress on his face. It was practically emanating from his pores. Part of her felt a tiny bit sorry for him. It was like going cold turkey. But there was nothing he could do.

She folded her arms across her chest. 'There is no Internet, Caleb. It's four weeks. Live with it.'

He took a deep breath and turned towards her. His brown eyes fixed on hers. It was the first time in for ever that he'd really looked at her. *Really* looked at her.

'What's going on with you, Addison?'

She blinked. 'What's going on with me? Are you serious?'

Why did every conversation feel as if it ended up as a fight?

'Yeah, I'm serious. I can't believe what you said to me back home.'

'And I can't believe you came home from work an hour before we were due to leave and thought you would tell me you weren't coming on holiday. At what point in your life did that seem okay to you?'

'Everything is a fight with you these days.'

He'd just echoed her thoughts. She thought this was all him. Was he trying to imply it was her too?

It lit a fuse in her. How dared he? Didn't he know what she'd just been told? Didn't he understand how worried she was?

Of course he didn't. She hadn't told him yet.

And at some point she'd need to.

Just not yet. Not until she knew.

She didn't want to tell him about the pregnancy. She didn't want to tell him about the scary news. She didn't need her husband to feel sorry for her. She needed him to love her. To love her enough to feel as if he could be there and support her.

Telling him about the pregnancy right now could make him tell her everything would be fine. And knowing Caleb, he'd probably think it would be. Then he'd go right home and start working hundred-hour weeks again.

She needed more than that. She needed more for this marriage.

'How can everything be a fight when you're never there?'

He sighed. 'You work too. There's been nights when you've been busy too. There have been events you've had to go to—people you've had to meet.'

She nodded her head. 'You're absolutely right. But the difference between you and me is that, when I know I'm going to be out at night, I make sure I've spent time with Tristan during the day.'

'That's easy for you to do.'

'Actually, it isn't. But I make the time.'

She bit her lip. Everything was a fight between them right now. And she hated that.

'Always fault-finding, always criticising. Can I ever do anything right in your eyes these days?'

And it looked as if this was going to become a fight too.

Trouble was, she was just too tired for this. She wasn't sure if it was the travel that had exhausted her, or the pregnancy. She could remember at this stage in her pregnancy with Tristan she'd come home from work and go straight to bed. In those days, Caleb would just come to bed with her.

She turned away. She just wanted to sleep now. She couldn't even be bothered changing out of her swimsuit.

'You gave me an ultimatum.' His voice was quiet, almost whispered. It was as if he was still getting over the shock. 'Why would you do that? It was just straight out of the blue.'

She stopped walking. Her hand was on the door. From here she could see that Tristan was already sleeping. She hadn't even got around to putting the DVD on. That was fine. She would just climb in next to him.

She kept her voice low too. 'It wasn't out of the blue, Caleb. This has been building for the last few years. We've slipped away from each other—we've lost each other...' her voice started to break '...and I've had enough. I can't live like this any more because I don't feel as if I'm living.'

She glanced over her shoulder. 'This is it for us, Caleb. I chose this place deliberately because I didn't want Tristan and I to compete with your work any more. Some people think this place is paradise. You? I think you've barely noticed. We came here because I wanted to see if we had anything left worth saving. Because right now—I just don't know.'

She took one final look. He looked as if she'd just punched him in the guts.

So she turned, and went to bed.

# CHAPTER THREE

CALEB COULDN'T SLEEP. He should be sleeping after twenty hours' travel and staying up since they'd arrived but after the conversation with Addison, sleep was nowhere near him.

It felt as if she'd stuck a knife into his chest and twisted it.

But more importantly it was obvious that she didn't think this marriage could be saved. How on earth had he reached this point? Had he been sleepwalking through life not to have noticed how his wife felt?

Tristan and Addison were sleeping in one of the double beds together. He'd tried to sleep in the other with no success. Then, he'd tried the bed in the water bungalow. But the gentle lap, lap of the water underneath had only kept his mind buzzing. In the end, he'd ended up on the beach.

They'd probably spent a fortune on this holiday and he was sleeping like a beach bum. But the air seemed stiller out here. And although there was still a background noise from the lapping waves, it didn't seem as amplified out here.

He couldn't sleep because he was gripped with panic. Panic that life as he knew it was just about to slip through his fingers.

Work was still preying on his mind. At one point in the middle of the night he'd actually opened his computer and started working on something. But after half an hour he'd realised the futility of his actions. By the time he'd got home Harry would have worked on another version of this. It made no sense for him to do the same thing. But that didn't stop his fingers drumming on the table in irritation.

He couldn't help it. Working had almost become a compulsion—an addiction. How sad was that?

He wasn't sure he even knew how to relax any more. Just sitting annoyed him. His brain constantly revolving, thinking about the work-related things he could be doing.

Part of him was angry at Addison for forcing this on him.

Part of him understood the point she was trying to make. If he had an Internet connection he probably wouldn't have seen the sun set or rise again. He probably wouldn't have watched the fishes swimming underneath the glass panel under the coffee table.

He probably wouldn't have had time to wonder what he could say to his wife to make her change her mind.

She seemed different. Distant. As if she had a hundred other things that she wasn't saying to him. And to be honest, what she'd already said felt like enough. He didn't know how he'd cope if she said any more.

A waiter appeared at the beach bungalow carrying a large tray. Breakfast. Was it that time already?

Caleb nodded as the man set the loaded tray down in the kitchen and left again. Eggs, bacon, croissants and breakfast cereal for Tristan. Addison must have pre-ordered all this. He glanced into the bedroom. They were still sleeping.

He jumped in the shower and quickly changed. He wasn't sure quite what Addison expected today. He hadn't paid enough attention; he didn't even know what there was to do around here.

He stood at the bedroom door for a minute. Even sleeping, she looked stressed. The bedclothes were all messed up and it was obvious she'd tossed and turned all night. That wasn't like her. Addison used to sleep like the dead. He used to joke that a marching band could come through their house in the middle of the night and she wouldn't hear it.

Tristan was lying halfway across his mother's chest in his superhero pyjamas. Caleb's heart gave a squeeze. When was the last time he'd had a chance to see them like this?

It had been too long. She was right about the Christmas carol stuff. He'd had every intention of being there. But just as he'd been about to leave he'd received an emergency call from Singapore. One of their investors had taken unwell and he'd been asked to contact the family urgently. It had taken fourteen phone calls to track down his son and by the time he'd finally left the office Tristan's concert was already finished. He'd sat in the car park outside, looking at the darkened building and cursing himself that he hadn't got there on time.

He walked over to the bed and gave Tristan a little shake. 'Hey, superhero. Wake up. It's breakfast time and we've got a beach to play on.'

Bing. Just like that he was wide awake. He jumped down from the bed and ran through to the bathroom. Addison's eyes flickered open. Just for a second she looked fine. Then, whatever it was that was on her mind seemed to come flooding in again. He could almost see the shutters coming down.

'Breakfast is here,' he said. 'I'll take Tristan through.'

She gave a nod and turned away, climbing out of the bed and slipping on her dressing gown. This wasn't how they used to wake up. Before Tristan, some days they hadn't got up at all. When Tristan was a baby they used to bring him in beside them in the morning. He'd coo and smile quite happily, with not a single bit of guilt that he'd kept them up most of the night.

But those days were long gone. Caleb got up at five these days and was in the office for six. He didn't even recognise the breakfast cereal sitting on the kitchen table. He picked it up and stared at it.

'My favourite!' shouted Tristan, pulling himself up onto one of the chairs. 'What's the toy?'

'Let's see,' said Caleb, sitting down next to him and opening the pack. A horrible plastic spider dropped out onto the table. Tristan let out a shriek and jumped up laughing. Caleb started laughing too. Within a few minutes the breakfast cereal was scattered everywhere and the bowls upturned as they played 'catch the spider'.

By the time he looked up Addison was standing in the doorway, watching Tristan and smiling. 'What's all this noise?'

Tristan lifted his prize. 'It was a spider this time, Mum!'

'Oh, no! Not a spider.' She came over to the table and sat around the other side. 'Well, I'm not sitting next to a spider.'

She stared at the covered plates for a second. It was almost as if the silver domes lost her in thought. But she blinked and removed them. The smell of bacon and eggs filled the room.

Caleb lifted up the cups and coffee pot and started pouring.

'Oh, no. I'm going to have lemon tea instead.'

He raised his eyebrows. 'But you love coffee.'

She shrugged. 'I'm on a health kick.'

He sat down opposite her and picked up his knife and fork. 'Skinny latte with sugar-free caramel, skinny extra shot macchiato.'

The edges of her lips started to turn upwards.

'Skinny cortado, skinny mocha cortado. Shall I keep going?'

She rolled her eyes as she poured boiling water into her cup and added a slice of freshly cut lemon.

'You know what they say—too much caffeine makes a girl cranky.'

He couldn't help but smile. There was definitely an atmosphere between them. How could there be anything else after what had happened? But things didn't seem quite so antagonistic this morning.

'This from a woman who had a state-of-the-art coffee machine installed in our kitchen because...' he leaned across the table towards her '...and I quote, "it's got to be cheaper than the ten cups I buy a day from the coffee shops".' He pointed to her cup. 'And now you're drinking tea?'

'A girl's entitled to change her mind.' The words came out like lightning—just the way Addison usually was. But as soon as she'd said them her face fell. Almost as if she realised how they could be interpreted.

Had Addison changed her mind about him?

Tristan chose that second to ping his plastic spider across the table and straight into Addison's cup.

'Yow!' She stood up as water splashed all over her. It was the first time he'd noticed she'd barely touched her breakfast.

She held her hand out towards Tristan. 'Let's go and get ready.' She looked up at Caleb. 'There's a kids' club every morning for a few hours. Playing with other kids will be good for him. He'll be back with us every afternoon.'

Work. It was the first thought that shot across his mind.

Addison walked away holding Tristan's hand, her outline silhouetted by the sun streaming through one of the windows. Her hair might be tied up in a funny knot on top of her head, and she didn't have a scrap of make-up on, but his wife was still a stunner.

So, why was it, when he knew Tristan would be gone every morning, his first thought had been he could work?

He leaned forward and put his head in his hands. Five years ago that absolutely wouldn't have been the first thought on his mind. His mind would probably have gone in a whole other direction.

He was embarrassed to admit that thought— even to himself.

He stood up and walked through to the bedroom. 'I'll take him.'

'What?' Addison looked surprised; she was pulling some clothes for Tristan out of the drawers.

'If you point me in the right direction, I'll take him to the kids' club. You can stay and get showered and dressed.'

'No.' It was out before he'd barely finished speaking. 'I mean… I haven't seen the kids' club yet. I want to check it out. To make sure I'm happy to leave him there.'

His annoyance flared. It was almost as if she didn't trust him to be able to do that. To take Tristan to the kids' club and make sure it was okay. But he tempered it down. The last thing he needed to do today was have another argument. He picked up the clothes she'd looked out. 'In that case, we'll do it together. I'll get Tristan dressed while you shower.'

She hesitated for second, then nodded. 'Okay, I'll be ready in ten minutes.'

She grabbed a dress and some underwear and headed into the bathroom, closing the door behind her.

It was the little things. The little things he was starting to notice. She didn't used to close the door when she showered. On past occasions he'd joined her.

But today, it felt like just another sign that Addison was shutting him out.

He sighed and dressed Tristan, taking him out to the beach when he was ready. But Tristan pointed to the clear blue sea. 'Can we see the fishes?'

'Sure.' Caleb took his hand and led him along the walkway and into the over-water bungalow. They pushed the coffee table away and lay down next to the glass panel. There was a small piece of coral underneath and it was alive with activity.

'What's that one, Dad? The red and white one? And what's the blue one? It looks like Dory. Do you think we'll see Nemo too?'

Caleb shook his head and stared down at the gorgeous brightly coloured fish. He didn't have a single clue what any of them were. A large one swam past right underneath their noses. It was turquoise blue with pink stripes and little dashes of yellow. It looked like a painting Tristan would do at nursery. It was followed by a few much smaller, zebra-striped fish.

'I like that one,' said Tristan. 'Can we give it a name?'

Caleb smiled. 'Sure we can. What will we call it?'

'Tristan,' he suggested.

Caleb tried not to laugh. 'We'll have to see if we can buy a book somewhere to tell us what all the fishes are.' He looked around. 'And there are lots of boats. Maybe one day we can swim along the coral reef and go snorkelling.'

'What's snokling?'

Caleb laughed. 'It's where you go under the water and breathe through a little tube. You have a pair of goggles on so you can see all the fishes.'

'We can go and swim with the fishes?' Tristan looked mesmerised.

'Sure we can. Daddy will find out how today.'

Tristan's innocent gaze narrowed. 'You won't forget?'

Something twisted inside him. That was what his four-year-old associated with him—Daddy always forgetting his promises?

'I won't forget,' he said quickly. It felt like a kick somewhere painful. There was something horrible and uncomfortable about his little boy asking him that question. It was one thing for Addison to call him on his misdeeds, it was quite another for his four-year-old.

But there was something else. His brain was still spinning. Review a contract, phone that client, check the small print on another contract, speak to their lawyer about an impending business deal. He moved uncomfortably and glanced around. His shoulders were tense. His little boy was playing around him and his mind was still full of work things. Work things he could do nothing about.

So why were they still there? Why were they still running through his brain? Why couldn't he just relax and spend time with his son? Was it possible he'd forgotten how to relax?

There was a movement out of the corner of his eye. Addison was standing in the doorway, carrying Tristan's backpack in one hand. She was wearing a short red sundress and had a pair of sunglasses on her head.

She knelt down next to them and pulled some suncream out of the backpack, slathering it over Tristan's skin as he squirmed. When she finished she pulled a baseball cap from the back-

pack and stuck it on his head. 'Right. Let's go
and see the kids' club.'

It was odd—walking away from a place and
not locking all the doors behind you.

They strolled up the path towards the main
resort. There was a variety of palm trees and
green bushes with the occasional burst of
bright red and orange flowers. The whole resort seemed to have been planned to perfection.

The kids' club was through the main reception and next to a small kids' pool. It was
shaded, with a variety of toys, ranging from
chalk boards, to racing cars, a complete tiny
wooden house and a table for arts and crafts.
There were four other kids all playing already
with two play leaders. One of the play leaders
came over straight away. 'Hi, I'm Kohia. Is this
Tristan?'

Tristan nodded. 'How did she know my name,
Mummy?'

Kohia knelt down. 'I know all the special
boys and girls that are coming to play here.'
She handed a clipboard to Addison. 'We need
you to answer a few questions about Tristan's
medical history, any allergies and likes and dis-
likes. After that we're good to go.'

Caleb looked around. Everything seemed
fine. The area was clean and tidy, the kids
looked happy and the play leaders seemed to

know what they were doing. Addison handed back the clipboard and waited a few minutes to make sure Tristan was settled. He was instantly distracted by a painting session at a nearby table. Kohia gave them a wave. 'Come back around one o'clock.'

Caleb glanced at his watch. Three and a half hours. What on earth would they do?

This morning had been strange. Caleb seemed in a better mood. He'd finally accepted there was no Internet or phone line and she hadn't seen him touch his computer at all. It felt like a miracle.

He was still on edge. They both were. But the tenseness in his muscles seemed to have dissipated a little. His shoulders weren't quite as tense but the furrows in his brow were still there. She could only imagine hers were the same.

Kohia shouted to them as they walked down the path. 'If you haven't tried the patisserie inside yet, you should definitely give it a go. The coconut cake is the best *ever*!'

Caleb turned towards her. 'Well, there's a recommendation. Why don't we give it a try when we've looked around?'

She gave a nod. She could sense his nerves

jangling again. Was he worried he might actually need to talk to her—spend time with her?

Her stomach gave a little lurch. She'd thought the other night that she might have fallen out of love with her husband. And that made her feel horrible. But it hadn't occurred to her that the same might have happened for him.

They walked in silence for a while, strolling through the tropical gardens. She'd never seen so many shades of green dotted with bright splashes of colour. Every now and then the foliage parted to give perfect views of the blue ocean and rolling sands. The resort complex was huge. There were five other beach bungalows like theirs, each with their own smaller over-water bungalow. Around the other side of the complex were twenty larger over-water bungalows with thatched roofs and a variety of walkways. The central hotel had four restaurants, three bars, a gym, training classes, a few shops, a spa and the huge, welcoming patisserie. The smell of coffee almost came to meet them.

She felt herself twitch. She craved it. She craved it so badly. She hadn't actually realised how much she loved it, or how much she drank. But as soon as she'd realised she was pregnant she'd switched to caffeine-free tea. She didn't want to take any chances with this baby. Not when the odds were apparently stacked against her anyway.

Caleb automatically walked in the direction of the patisserie, his eyes drawn to a huge glass cabinet packed with a variety of cakes.

'Skinny caramel latte?' She shook her head again.

'I'll have green tea.' She drifted along the edge of the glass cabinet just as her stomach gave a telltale rumble.

Caleb pointed to the cakes. 'Which one do you want?' He turned towards her, a quizzical look on his face. 'You didn't eat much this morning at all. You must be starving.'

She was. She'd been unsettled at breakfast and she didn't think it was anything to do with her pregnancy. Morning sickness had never been a problem before. It was most likely just the state of her life and the decisions she'd need to make.

She licked her lips as she looked at the labels on the cakes. She pointed to the coconut cake. Four layers of sponge with jam and coconut cream frosting. She didn't even want to think about the calories. Since she'd hardly had any breakfast—or eaten much on the flights yesterday—she figured it would all work out. 'I'll have a piece of that. What about you?'

Caleb had never been a cake kind of guy. But

he pointed towards another cabinet. 'I'll have a piece of peach pie. And a cappuccino.' He placed the orders and carried the tray outside to a terrace with a thatched roof and comfortable chairs.

Addison sat down. The view over the ocean was picture perfect and stretched on for miles and miles. There wasn't a single thing on the water in front of them. Although the temperature was warm, a gentle breeze blew off the ocean.

As he set the tray down and unloaded the food and drinks, again she got a little whiff of coffee. She could kill for a coffee right now. And poor Caleb would be right in the firing line.

Maybe now was the time to tell him about the pregnancy? It wouldn't take him long to notice that she wasn't drinking alcohol either. But would he join up the dots?

Something was stopping her. As soon as she told him he would immediately talk about plans for the future. She didn't want to do that. Not until she knew what she was doing. Not until she knew if she would be with him, or without him.

There were three other women sitting at a table behind them. She could see the admiring glances they were throwing in Caleb's direction. She was used to them. Caleb always got a second glance. With his deep brown eyes, dark hair and muscular build he was handsome. He filled out his clothes well. In around two days he'd have a killer tan too. But it wasn't a tan she worried about. It was the lines that had appeared on his forehead and around his eyes these last few years. It was the fact he permanently looked tired and as if he were thinking about three different things at once. It was the fact she didn't even feel, when she talked to him, that she was the actual focus of his attention.

That had to change. It had to. Or this relationship would just come to a sad end. Did she really want that to happen?

Caleb sat down and started sipping his coffee. He gave her a careful smile. 'If I know you, any minute now you'll start to have coffee withdrawals and you'll leap across the table like a snarling wolf and grab my coffee.'

He hadn't noticed she'd been off it for weeks now, but then, he was never around.

She gave a nod. 'I could do. So beware. You never know when I'll pounce.' She lifted her fork. 'But in the meantime I'm going to focus on having some sinful calories.' She dug her fork into the four layers of cake. One forkful told her all she needed to know. 'Hmm, gorgeous.'

'Thank you,' came the cheeky reply. 'You're not so bad yourself.'

She couldn't help but smile. This was the Caleb she used to know. The one who found it easy to make quick quips.

She leaned over and speared a bit of his peach pie.

'Hoy!' His hand had been hovering just above the plate.

'You're too slow,' she joked. 'If you're not fast, you're last.'

As she put the pie into her mouth a bit of the syrup on the peaches dripped down her chin.

Caleb laughed and leaned forward. 'Can't take you anywhere.' He had a paper napkin in his hand and he caught the drip before it landed on her dress. But as he pulled his hand away his fingers caught the underside of her chin.

She froze. When was the last time he'd actually touched her face like that? She couldn't even remember. She swallowed the pie quickly and picked up her plate. 'Here, you try mine.'

But Caleb had caught the moment too. He was looking at her and it took him a few seconds to move. He picked up his fork. 'If it isn't as good as she said, can we demand a refund?' He took a piece of the cake. 'I take it back. It's delicious.'

He leaned back in his chair and looked out over the ocean, sipping his coffee. 'Why did you pick here?'

It was the first time he'd asked that. She didn't think he'd paid much attention at all when she'd told him about the holiday.

She sighed. 'It's been three years since we've had a holiday. I don't actually think we've had a week off together in all that time—just a few days here and there.' She glanced out over the ocean too. 'I told the travel agent I wanted somewhere warm, quiet and luxurious that catered for kids. She'd been here on her honeymoon, so she recommended it.'

He nodded. 'Well, they've got the luxury part right. But it's not too stuffy either. It's quite relaxed.'

She raised her eyebrows. 'Relaxed. There's a word you don't recognise.'

He gave her the look. The one that told her he wasn't going to say out loud what was in his head right now.

'How are things at your work?'

She briefly pressed her lips together as she played with her cup. 'Things are good. It's busy. The conference for next year is booked. The advertising campaign is sorted. We've got about twenty interviews lined up with the national newspapers. And I'm meeting the medical director from St Peter's hospital in a few weeks.'

'Why's that?' He looked curious.

'Because one of the consultant gynaecologists

there said we weren't allowed to display our posters about ovarian cancer. It would frighten the patients.'

She could see Caleb trying to choke back his indignation.

She nodded. 'Right there with you. That's why I've bypassed him completely and arranged to meet the medical director.' She took another breath. 'In fact, I've been so busy, that I've been thinking about hiring someone else.'

Caleb had started eating his pie again and looked up. 'Another admin assistant?'

She tried to pick her words. She wasn't ready to tell him everything so that made this kind of awkward. 'No. Another me.'

He put down his fork. 'What do you mean another you?'

She picked at her cake. Anything was better than looking at him right now. Caleb's gaze could be intense. Particularly if he thought you were hiding something—and it had been a long time since she'd done that.

She tried to keep things light. 'I'd be looking for someone who could job share with me. Lara is great and I definitely want to keep her, but Tristan only has another year before school. He's already at nursery. I want to spend as much time with him as I can.'

And with our new baby, she thought silently to herself.

She finally met his gaze. 'I feel a bit guilty. I had Tristan just as the whole charity thing exploded. I probably should have done this right from the start. But it's difficult then—when everything is new—and you don't really realise how much work it will entail. I feel like I've missed out.' She bit her lip. 'Like we've both missed out.'

He shifted in his chair.

'It's time for me to re-evaluate. And this is part of what I think I should do. When we get home I'm going to put the advert out. It's hard to let things go—I get that and I don't really want to do it. But, at the end of the day, it doesn't need to be me that does everything.' She waved her hand. 'If I get hit by a bus in London, or hit by a speedboat here, someone else will step in. The charity won't disappear. Someone else will do what needs to be done.'

It hadn't been as hard to say out loud as she thought. And while she might have been talking about her own business, she knew that everything she'd just said could be reflected in Caleb and his business for the last three years too. And it was clear he knew that. He had that frown again and she could see the tension across his neck and shoulders.

'Sounds like you re-evaluated a whole lot more than your business in these thoughts.'

She bristled. She hadn't said anything about them. But she could hardly deny it. They had actually been much more of a focus than the business.

'At any point did you think to talk to me?' His tone was accusing.

One of the women at the nearby table looked around.

Addison leaned forward and kept her voice low. 'How can I talk to you when you're never there?'

Frustration was building inside her. For a few moments this morning she'd wondered if they could start to mend bridges. Now it seemed they were right back to where they'd started.

Could she really do this for the next four weeks? Maybe she should just tell him every-thing and see if they could survive the next four weeks.

Caleb sighed and sat back in his chair. She didn't want to fight. She didn't have the energy to fight.

After a few moments he spoke again. 'Tristan loved the fish. I want a chance to get him in the water and maybe see some. I think that part of the lagoon looks quite shallow. I'm going to ask at Reception if there are any scuba-diving trips that are family friendly. What do you think?'

They were back to safer waters. Maybe he didn't want to fight either. And at least he was making an effort for them to do something together as a family. She nodded. 'I think he'll love that. There's also a boat trip around the island we could do and a place we can hire bikes for the day.'

'You on a bike, really? I've never seen you on a bike.'

'And I've never seen you on one either. But no wonder. It's a death wish with the traffic in London. Here—there's hardly any cars. It might be fun.'

Fun. There was a word she hadn't heard in a while. That was what she wanted for Tristan. Fun.

One of the hotel staff walked past and handed them a leaflet. 'Just in case you didn't see our sign in Reception. We screen movies on our private beach. Tonight's movie is *Sliding Doors*. Come along and enjoy—the staff will be there to serve cocktails.'

Addison picked up the flyer and wrinkled her nose. '*Sliding Doors*? Lara mentioned that to me.'

'When?'

'When she turned up at the door crying. She

said she'd had a *Sliding Doors* moment. I didn't know what she meant.'

He leaned a bit closer. 'You've never seen the movie?'

She shook her head.

'I can't believe that. You'd love it. We'll need to see if we can get Tristan settled in bed tonight. If we do, we can watch the film.'

Addison nodded. She couldn't remember the last time she'd watched a grown-up film. Her last cinema visits had all been with Tristan to see some kind of kids' cartoon-style film. Some of them had been good and some of them had almost sent her to sleep.

Caleb gave a little smile. 'I wonder how Lara and Reuben are getting on.'

Addison shuddered. 'I can't imagine. I can't believe you never told me you'd agreed to let him stay. At least I could have warned her.'

'There's no need to warn her about Reuben. He's a good guy. He'll look after her.'

'Reuben Tyler? A good guy? That'll explain why I walked in on him punching you.'

Caleb shook his head. 'That was nothing. It was guy stuff. And I was partly to blame.'

'How?'

'Reuben doesn't really believe in happy ever afters. He doesn't really believe that love exists. And I called him on it that night. His parents' relationship isn't exactly ideal. When that's the example you've seen all your life it can have a real effect.'

'So he punched you?'

'What's a punch between friends? You didn't hang around to see the rest. He was sorry. He was instantly sorry. But you've never really given him a chance—you can't see past the punch.'

She shifted in her chair. It might be a little true. 'When you see someone punching the man you love it kind of puts you off them for life.' She looked up at him. 'Why have you never told me this about him before?'

He looked a bit uncomfortable. 'Reuben's a private kind of guy. He doesn't like his life being reviewed.'

'But we've never kept secrets from each other.'

He met her gaze. 'It wasn't my secret—it was his. Look, Reuben has good points. You just haven't had a chance to see them. We've been friends since school and I trust him—I'll always trust him. Lara is in safe hands. Don't doubt it. Ask her when we get back.'

'I'm just praying I don't get back and find a note with her written notice because she's not been able to stand sharing a house with Reuben.'

'No way. I'd take bets on it. Reuben can be a real charmer.'

'And that's supposed to reassure me? I think that actually makes me feel worse.'

He rolled his eyes. 'I promise you, they'll be fine.'

'Well, she has no way to get in touch. I'll just need to wait and see.'

One of the hotel staff passed by and picked up their dishes.

It was odd. He felt nervous. Tristan had gone to bed like a dream. The hotel staff had given them a monitor so they would hear if he wakened, leaving them free to sit outside on the beach and watch the film.

The screen had been set up just a little way down the beach from their bungalow. A number of other guests had arrived and had already staked out their space on the sand. Waiters came back with brightly coloured cocktails as the sun set in the sky and the purples turned to dark blue.

Caleb paced about the kitchen. It almost felt like going on a first date. Which was ridiculous. They'd known each other for ten years.

He would always remember his first sight of her. Nervously laughing at a charity event, wearing a bright pink dress, glittery sandals and a sash that said *Ask me about ovarian cancer*.

So he had. Her blonde hair had been curly

then, sitting in ringlets around her face and bouncing on her shoulders. He'd been struck by the sincerity in her clear green eyes as she'd told him about her sister and ovarian cancer and what she was doing to try and raise the profile of the disease.

And when she'd stood on her tiptoes and asked him in a whisper if she was doing okay he'd fallen in love instantly. And that had been that.

He hadn't been able to contain himself. He'd wanted to see her every day. His family had loved her almost as instantly as he had and they'd all helped over the years supporting the work of her charity.

They'd waited a few years to get married. His business had been doing really well at that point and when he'd handed her the keys to their new house in Belgravia she'd almost choked.

When she'd walked down the aisle on their wedding day in her slim, cream fitted gown her eyes had widened in shock at the amount of good friends he'd managed to fly in from around the world. It had been a logistical nightmare but her mum and dad had helped a lot. Friends from the US, Australia, France and Denmark had all attended the wedding and she'd been delighted. The expense and effort had been worth it for the expression on her face alone.

It seemed such a long time ago.

Addison came out of the bedroom. She had a full-length blue patterned dress on and a pair of flat sandals.

'Have you got the monitor?'

He nodded and held up his hand.

'Should we take something to sit on for the beach?'

'I've had a look. They've got big blankets on the beach already. We just need to find one to sit on.'

She gave a nod and had a final check on Tristan, planting a kiss on his forehead before she finally came back out. She took a deep breath. 'Okay, let's go.'

They walked along the beach. It was cooler than during the day, but still warm, even though the sun had set. They settled on a blanket near the screen and a waiter appeared instantly to take their order.

Caleb didn't even need to ask. Addison loved cocktails. Even if she hadn't wanted to see the film, he'd bet she would have come along for the cocktails.

'A strawberry daiquiri for my wife and I'll have whatever the local speciality is.'

Addison gave a weird kind of smile and jumped up as the waiter walked away, catching his arm and saying something in a low voice to him. The waiter looked at her with a smile and left.

'What's wrong?'

She shook her head. 'Nothing. It's just that some places put mint leaves in the strawberry daiquiri and I don't like them. I was asking him to leave them out.'

He wrinkled his nose. 'Do they? I don't remember that.'

She gave him a nudge. 'That's because you don't drink enough of them.'

There was something about the way she did it. The way she said it.

One thing that Addison had never been was a fake. And all of a sudden he got the strangest sensation. She wasn't being entirely truthful. Was it the nudge, the joke?

He settled back on the blanket and tried to put it out of his mind. Addison sat next to him without touching. She pulled her knees up to her chin and wrapped her arms around them as the film started.

He couldn't believe how uncomfortable he felt. Any time in the past he'd been this close to Addison he'd been touching her. His arm was literally itching right now to move around her shoulders and pull her closer. But since her ultimatum he hadn't felt sure about anything.

He glanced around at all the other couples

spread out across the beach. Some were lying completely flat on their blankets, staring at the giant screen. Others were side by side. But all were touching. All looked like they were couples. Him and Addison?

He moved. He shifted over on the blanket so his legs were touching hers. She didn't flinch. She didn't jump away. He waited a few seconds then put his arm around her shoulders. A few seconds later he pulled her closer.

She shifted into a more comfortable position, putting her head against his shoulder, and he finally let out the breath he'd been holding.

'I can't believe you haven't seen this film,' he whispered. 'It's a chick flick.'

'Oh, well, if it's a chick flick I must have seen it.'

'Well, it's right up there with *Dirty Dancing* and *Pretty Woman*, except, of course, it's British. Actually, it's really quite good. You'll like it.'

The waiter appeared back with their drinks. 'The strawberry daiquiri for the lady, and a Bora Bora Delight for the gentleman. Enjoy. Give me a wave if you want a refill.'

Caleb took a drink of the yellow and orange concoction. The rum hit the back of his throat straight away, quickly followed by a burst of orange liqueur and a hint of coconut.

'Wow, take a sip of this.'

For a second she looked as though she might actually say no, then she gave a little nod and took the glass and straw in her hand, taking a sip. 'Lovely,' she said.

'Hits you right in the back of the throat, doesn't it?' She gave a smile and handed it back.

'I'll stick with my strawberry daiquiri,' she said quickly. 'I'd be drunk in five minutes if I took one of those.' She settled her head back on his shoulder.

And, for the first time since the holiday had begun, Caleb finally started to relax.

This was getting awkward. Things would be so much simpler if she could just tell him the truth.

Trouble was, apart from all the emotional stuff, there was the practical stuff too. Caleb would immediately want to get online and find out everything possible about the NT test and the type of results you could get.

She'd done a quick five-minute search at the airport. That was enough. She'd closed her phone down. She didn't need to be bamboozled by everything else. What Dr Mackay had told her was enough. She'd been given a set of odds.

Odds that she had to accept because she was having this baby.

She shifted a little on the beach rug. Caleb's

arm was draped around her shoulders. It felt good there. It felt comforting, even though he had no idea what he was comforting her about.

She was quite sure he hadn't noticed anything yet. Her pregnancy wasn't obvious. Her breasts were bigger and her waist had thickened. All things that could be easily hidden in beach dresses and palazzo pants. In her bikini it might not be so easy to hide. Thank goodness she'd packed some swimsuits and a variety of sarongs.

She hadn't known quite what excuse to make when Caleb had ordered her a cocktail. The waiter had given a pleasant nod when she'd asked him to leave the daiquiri out of the strawberry daiquiri. She'd just need to make sure they used the same waiter again.

The film was getting interesting. A time split. In one version she missed the Tube. In the second she caught it and got home to find her boyfriend in bed with another woman. Now she understood what Lara had meant when she'd said she'd had a *Sliding Doors* moment. Now it made perfect sense.

She could feel the heat emanating from Caleb's body. His arm moved slightly, his fingers at the back of her neck. She gave a little groan. She loved that. She loved that light, tickling feeling at the back of her neck. It totally and utterly re-

laxed her. She could let him do this for hours—
and he knew that.

As the film progressed her mind started to
spin. Two different versions of the same life.
What if that was her?

If someone could give her a flash forward
into the future, one with Caleb and one without,
which would she pick? Which one would be best
for her? Best for Tristan and best for the baby?

She took another sip of her cocktail. Cocktails
weren't quite so good without the alcohol. But it
would be around another year before she could
get the real thing again. This would have to do.

Caleb leaned a bit closer. 'You enjoying this?
I told you it was a good film.'

She smiled as a sea breeze blew past, carrying the scent of Caleb's aftershave with it. It was
different. It was different from the one he normally wore to work every day. And yet it was
familiar. She'd bought it for him on honeymoon
years before.

Something stirred inside her. He'd bought
another one of these? When had he done that?
Surely that must mean something?

She kept watching the film. All the way
through hoping the heroine would have one life,
then, after the twist at the end, realising she had
to live the other. Nothing was simple. Life was
completely complicated.

A tear slid down her cheek.

'Hey,' said Caleb. 'It's meant to be a happy ending. Just a little—different.'

She wiped the tear away as they stood up. He kept his arm around her as they walked back down the beach to the bungalow.

'That was good, wasn't it? We'll see what they have in store for tomorrow night.'

'Sure.' Her stomach was starting to churn a little as they walked through the doors of the bungalow. She wasn't quite sure what came next.

But Caleb just dropped a kiss on her head and walked off to the bedroom.

She felt a little wave of relief. And then a little pang of regret.

Shouldn't her husband be trying to persuade her to join him?

The relaxation of the night felt ruined. She snuck in next to Tristan and tossed and turned all night.

# CHAPTER FOUR

FOR A TIME last night, Caleb had felt as if things were almost normal.

Or they would be if there weren't this strange vibe between them.

It felt as if his wife was hiding something from him. He'd never felt like this before. Or maybe he just hadn't noticed how things were with Addison? And that made him feel even guiltier.

Since she'd issued him with the ultimatum he'd noticed *everything*.

Every passing expression on her face. The times she looked as if she might say something but then just pressed her lips together.

The physical stuff too. If she gave the tiniest flinch or shudder. The way she wore her hair, or her clothes. Her attentiveness to Tristan. The far-off look in her eyes sometimes.

But the thing that he noticed most was the aura of sadness around her.

Even when she laughed and smiled it was still there.

And that was like a tight fist squeezing around the muscles of his heart.

Was it him? Had he done this to her?

Please no.

His mind was starting to play tricks on him. Addison had always spoken her mind. But, the ultimatum, must have been building inside her for some time. Which meant she hadn't been speaking her mind to Caleb.

He could remember lots of conversations—or parts of conversations—when she'd mentioned things he'd forgotten—or things he should remember. The irony almost killed him.

Maybe he was naïve, but he couldn't think of a single thing that Addison couldn't tell him. And that was when his mind started playing tricks on him.

Had she met someone else? Was that what all this was about? Had she developed feelings for someone else and she was trying this holiday to see how she still felt about this marriage?

That lit a fire inside him, a burning rage. He couldn't bear the thought of Addison with someone else. But she'd never been that type of person, so why would she do that now?

But what else could it be? She couldn't possibly have murdered someone. She wouldn't have done anything illegal. Could it be business re-lated? The charity could be in trouble. But she'd told him she was going to hire someone else—that just wouldn't fit.

Was there any chance that Addison could have money worries? Maybe she was one of those secret spenders that ran up credit cards without telling anyone and couldn't pay them off? Ridiculous. Their bank account was more than healthy.

Bottom line was he couldn't think of a single reason for his wife to be so down. To be so upset. To be so frustrated.

For the first time in the last few years he didn't want to think about work. He didn't want to think about business. He wanted to think about his family. He wanted to think about his wife.

It was the second morning he'd seen the sunrise. Lots of red, oranges and peaches lighting up the sky. Bora Bora was definitely one of the most beautiful places on Earth.

He glanced at his watch. Reception would be opened by now. He could do what he needed to.

By the time he came back the waiter had just arrived with breakfast. He went through to wake up Tristan and Addison.

'Come on, guys, breakfast time. We have some plans today.'

'We do?' Addison sat up in bed and rubbed her sleepy eyes.

'I've booked us on a circle boat tour of the island. We get to meet some rays and sharks. And I've changed Tristan to an afternoon slot for the kids' club.'

Addison looked surprised. 'Oh, okay. I guess we better get up, then.'

They washed their faces and hands and came through for breakfast. At least she ate something this morning. A croissant with butter and jam and another cup of lemon tea.

It didn't take them long to get ready. While Addison showered and changed he plastered Tristan in suncream and looked out the strange all-in-one swimsuit she had for him, and the baseball cap with the flappy bit at the back of the neck.

She came out of the bathroom with a long pink dress on, her swimming costume straps visible underneath. She was carrying a floppy hat and some sunglasses. 'Oh, great, I was just about to do that.'

She gave him a wary glance. 'I'm not sure how I feel about swimming with sharks or rays.' Then she shook her head. 'Actually, that's not true. I'm entirely sure how I feel about swimming with sharks and rays.'

He laughed. 'Don't worry. I'm sure it's perfectly safe or they wouldn't do it. Let's just wait until we're there and see how you feel then.'

'I get to swim with a shark?' Tristan was astounded.

Caleb laughed and swung him up onto his shoulders. 'Maybe. We'll see what we think.' He bent down and grabbed the bucket and spade. 'Let's take these too. I'm sure we'll stop at a beach somewhere and we'll get to build a castle.'

It didn't take them long to reach the boat. It was even better than he'd hoped for—a traditional Tahitian outrigger canoe made of polished wood for ten people with a motor attached.

Addison looked a little wary. 'That's what we're going in?' she whispered. He nodded and handed her and Tristan the life jackets that everyone was required to wear.

'I thought it might be fun to see the island the traditional way. We don't need to paddle. They have a motor, but I think the guides might do a bit of paddling.'

One of the guides came over to meet them and check their life jackets. He stood in the shallow waters and helped them into the boat. Although it looked small it was actually quite comfortable and there was nothing like being on the perfect crystal-blue lagoon waters. Another few tourists joined them and they set off.

From the lagoon they could admire the tower-ing, rocky, green summit of Mount Otemanu.

Addison was sitting directly in front of him with her camera in her hand. He leaned forward. 'The colours here seem unreal, don't they?'

She gave a nod and leaned back a little to-wards him. The dazzling blue of the lagoon was enhanced by the green of the palm trees and white sandy beaches. Every turn of the head gave a different view. And every single view was like a perfect painting.

As they crossed the lagoon they could see a variety of tropical fish swimming beneath them. After a while the boat pulled up on one of the private beaches of a *motus* and the guides picked fresh fruit from the trees for them.

They stayed there for an hour, eating the fruit and some freshly prepared fish. Caleb used the extra time to build sandcastles with Tristan. For a four-year-old he was serious. He knew ex-actly what he wanted his creation to look like and wasted no time in telling his father exactly what to do.

Addison was sitting on the beach with her legs curled under her, watching them. After a while she called Tristan over and whispered in his ear.

Tristan shot Caleb a mischievous look. 'That sounds like a good idea.'

Caleb knew when he was being set up. 'What's going on?'

Addison smiled as she stood. 'Oh, nothing. I was just telling Tristan that my favourite memory of being on a beach as a child was when me and my sister buried my dad up to his neck in the sand.'

Tristan didn't need to be told twice. He'd already started digging in the sand with his plastic spade with an enthusiasm that made Caleb laugh. The guides and fellow tourists all laughed and joined in too. Caleb walked over and slung his arm around Addison's shoulders. 'There's no getting out of this, is there?'

She gave him a wide smile. 'Not a chance.'

It was the first time he felt she'd genuinely smiled since they'd got there. She seemed more relaxed today, more at ease. And if getting buried up to his neck in the sand could make her laugh, he would do it—every day for the rest of his life.

It was amazing what a bit of teamwork could do. It wasn't long before Tristan jumped up and down and shouted him over. Caleb looked at the hole. It wasn't quite deep enough, but if he went on his knees he could be buried up to his neck.

Addison was trying to hide her laughter. But she wasn't doing a good job. He jumped straight in the hole. 'Come on, guys, do your worst.'

The sand quickly filled up around him. It wasn't too tight and wasn't too heavy. Tristan pushed as much sand in as he could. He couldn't contain his excitement and it was probably the cutest thing Caleb had ever seen. As the sand came around his neck Addison came over with her camera in hand.

'Come on, Tristan, let's get a picture of you next to this big head in the sand.'

'Who are you saying has a big head?'

'Oh, that would always be you,' she quipped back as she snapped away.

The others snapped away too. 'Come on,' shouted one of the tour guides with a wink. 'Let's all get back on the boat.'

Addison held out her hand to Tristan. 'Let's go, honey. We need to see if there are more fish.'

Tristan's head flicked between Caleb, trapped in the sand, and the boat, which everyone else was climbing on. He dragged behind his mother walking slowly.

Caleb started shouting. 'You can't leave me here. What if a crocodile comes out of the water and eats me?'

Tristan's eyes widened. 'There are crocodiles?'

The guide shook his head. 'No. There aren't any crocodiles.' He leaned down and whispered not so quietly in Tristan's ear, 'But there are giant octopi that can crawl out the sea and swallow someone whole.'

Tristan's mouth fell open. 'But what about Daddy?' he asked.

The guide turned to the people on the boat. 'Should we let him back out?'

One of the other tourists shrugged. 'We might need him. If the motor breaks we might need help rowing home.'

Addison was watching the whole thing with a smile on her face.

The guide gave a little nod then. He waved his arm. 'Okay, then, folks. Everybody back out. The octopi aren't getting fed today.'

Caleb waited patiently for them to dig him back out. Being buried in the sand was surprisingly cool. But his head was warm. And sand had got into places that sand shouldn't get into.

Digging out took longer than digging in. But after ten minutes he was out, shaking sand off his clothes and picking up his baseball boots. Tristan ran over and gave him a bear hug and his heart gave a little surge.

When was the last time he'd been his son's hero?

That made him uncomfortable. Every father should be their son's hero. He'd just let other things get in the way. He swung Tristan up into his arms and made his way back over to the out-rigger canoe.

As they waited to climb back on board he took a deep breath and looked around. This really was like a little piece of paradise. He couldn't, for one second, think of any other people he'd want to be here with.

Tristan and Addison were his whole world.

He'd forgotten about the feel of his little boy's arms around his neck. Tristan was brushing some sand out of Caleb's hair and laughing. Then, he immediately started talking about his favourite wrestlers. Caleb smiled. He'd heard these stories time and time again. But when was the last time he'd actually listened?

He gave Tristan a tickle. 'You honestly think Cena could take The Rock? Not a chance. Not ever.'

He spun around. Addison was leaning against a palm tree watching them and waiting for her turn to board.

There was something about her expression on her face. She didn't look happy or sad, just thoughtful—the way she'd looked a lot in the last few days.

She blinked and realised he was staring at her. She gave a little shake, then gave them a wave and walked back over. She tapped her camera. 'I think I have all the blackmail material that I'll need.'

Caleb groaned. 'How much is this going to cost me?'

She shrugged. 'Maybe another piece of cake. There was a chocolate one I've got my eye on.'

One of the tourist guides held out his hand to help Addison on the boat. She picked up the skirts of her dress, giving him a little flash of her legs.

He smiled. He hadn't pursued her last night—even though he'd wanted to. They were at a strange kind of impasse. She hadn't seemed so angry, or so reserved. But he hadn't wanted to cross any lines.

He hadn't banked on having to win back his wife. Especially when he hadn't realised he'd almost lost her.

He'd been angry at her at first, taking him away from the business he loved. The fact he had no Internet or phone access literally made him twitch.

But he was beginning to get a little perspective. How many hours a week had he actually been working? When was the last time he'd sat on the sofa with Tristan and watched some cartoons? And when was the last time he'd spent an evening solely with his wife?

The tour guide waved them over and he and

Tristan climbed back on board. Tristan couldn't contain himself. He kept hanging over the side.

'What are you doing, little guy?'

Tristan grinned. 'I'm looking for crocodiles and octopuses.'

Caleb nodded. 'And can you see any?'

'Not yet. But I'm going to keep looking.'

The canoe moved off. There was no one else around; they had this whole piece of the ocean to themselves. The crystal-blue waters stretched out as far as the eye could see, merging with the pale blue sky and white clouds. As they ventured further around the island a little speck of red appeared on the horizon—a windsurfer. It was like a scene from a postcard or a travel brochure.

The tour guide started talking. 'We're coming up on the shallow waters where we'll go swimming with sharks and rays. I'll give you all some instructions before you go in the water.' He gave them all a wink. 'And don't worry, I haven't lost a tourist yet.'

Addison leaned forward and whispered in his ear. 'Not a chance. Not a blooming chance.'

He leaned his head back. 'Addison Connor, are you scared?'

He was baiting her. He knew he was. But it always worked with Addison.

She hit his shoulder. 'Don't you start on me, sand boy.'

She sat back again. Her hands were gripping her bag just a little too tightly. He leaned back and put his hand on her leg. 'Hey, I'm happy to take one for the Connor team. You and Tristan can take pictures if you want.'

Her head gave the slightest nod.

'Look, Daddy!' Tristan's voice was full of wonder and the tourist guide started to laugh.

'Well, as our young friend has already noticed, this is where the wildlife come to meet us.' He waved his hand. 'Look around you.'

He pointed across the clear waters. 'Blacktip reef sharks, stingrays and sergeant major fish.'

It was like something from a film. The first blacktip reef sharks appeared before the boat had even come to a complete stop.

As the guide worked to tie them off to an anchored buoy, a half-dozen or so of the five-foot-long sharks swam in slow circles nearby, along with several stingrays and a school of yellow-and-black-striped sergeant major fish. Caleb felt as if he were in the middle of a giant aquarium.

The sharks weren't shy. They came up and nudged the canoe.

The guide laughed and jumped in the water. 'We come here every day. Blacktip sharks normally stay around coral reefs and shallow waters. They are generally quite timid, but they've got used to us. They eat other small fishes.'

Addison's eyes were following the stingrays. 'What about them?'

'They're docile too. They just don't like to be stood on. But I'll make sure there are none on the ocean floor before you all get in.'

Several of the others tourists were already stripping off their clothes. Caleb did the same. He shed his T-shirt and shorts quickly until he was down to just his swimming shorts.

'Wait,' said Addison as she rummaged through her bag. She pulled out a bottle of sunscreen. 'Turn around until I spray some of this on your back. You don't want to get burned.'

He turned around and winced as the spray hit his back. How come these sprays were always cold?

Next minute he felt the warmth of Addison's palm on his back. Both palms. He sucked in a breath.

She'd been so distant. And what she was doing right now was an everyday thing. But having Addison's palms massaging his back didn't feel like an everyday thing. It felt a whole lot more than that.

Her movements weren't sensual, they were brisk, perfunctory. Rubbing in suncream was second nature to Addison.

She finished with a little slap on his back. 'All done.'

He smiled and jumped overboard into the waist-high water. The water was warm and inviting. Tristan leaned over and stuck his hands in just as the shoal of yellow-and-black-striped sergeant major fish swam past.

'Woo-hoo! Look, Mummy, look at the fish.'

Caleb held his hands out towards him. 'Want to jump in next to Dad? I'll hold you.'

Tristan jumped up and down, rocking the canoe. He could see a flash of mad panic in Addison's eyes. 'You want to take him in with sharks and stingrays?'

He nodded. 'You heard the guides. They haven't lost a tourist yet. It's safe. Let's give him a chance to see them. He'll probably never get this chance again. It's only for a few minutes.'

He could see Addison suck in a deep breath. The rest of the tourists were in the water, touching the sharks and stingrays around them. The guides were showing them what to do.

He kept Tristan in his arms, with his little legs wrapped around his waist. The guides were fantastic. The sharks and rays seemed comfortable around the people. They swam around, occasionally bumping against them. But never in a way that made him concerned.

Addison finally relaxed a little, taking out her

camera and snapping pics of them both. They ended up being in the water for much longer than he'd planned. It was so tranquil. The experience of being this close to the creatures was just too good an opportunity. The whole time that the tourists were in the water the guides gave them a rundown of the different species and how they lived. They emphasised the importance of the coral reefs and natural habitats for the creatures and things that could threaten their existence. Caleb had never really experienced anything like this before.

And it was so much better because of the people he was with.

Addison finally plucked up the courage to stick her toes in the water but that was it. She snapped away taking pictures of Tristan and Caleb together in the water.

After a while he grabbed the camera back and snapped a few pictures of her sitting on the canoe. He took a quick glance before he handed it back. Addison was as beautiful as ever, the floppy hat on her head and in her long pink sundress. She didn't have her glasses on and—it couldn't be hidden—there was still something in her eyes. An inherent sadness that he just couldn't get to the bottom of. They had to talk. They had to sit down and actually *talk*.

A little wash of guilt swept over him. Could

they talk? Could he actually tell her that he already had a pile of CVs in his drawer of potential employees?

Could he tell her he'd deliberately been putting things off because—in a way—his work was his escape?

If he was at work, he didn't need to tell his wife why he wasn't keen to have another child. A child that he actually longed for.

Right now the irony killed him. He'd spent time avoiding Addison because he couldn't tell her what he feared—that if they had another child she might slip away from him again. It turned out his wife had been slipping away from him the whole time anyway.

The conversation from a year ago had never left him. The disappointment on her face about not considering another child. He'd avoided every opportunity to discuss it—and that hadn't exactly helped the atmosphere at home. The one and only time he'd tried to talk to her about how she'd felt after having Tristan—she'd brushed him off. She'd made light of how down she'd been. It was almost as if her head wouldn't let her acknowledge that again. It made him think she might be just as afraid as he was. Which was why he'd left things and the tension had built.

But today had felt different. Today had felt

good. He'd actually been relaxed—really relaxed. He hadn't let work thoughts plague his mind at all. He couldn't remember the last time that had happened.

The heat of the day started to build as the canoe made its way back over the lagoon towards their resort. It was a relief to get back into the main building and the air conditioning.

Tristan bounded off to join the rest of the children at the kids' club. His energy was incredible.

Caleb turned to Addison. 'Chocolate cake?'

She shook her head. 'Not yet, maybe later. Let's take a walk. I'd like to see a little of Bora Bora outside of the resort.'

He nodded. 'Sure. Give me five minutes to change. I've got sand in difficult places.'

She laughed and nodded. 'Okay, I'll get us something cool to drink.'

Addison watched as Caleb crossed the reception area of the resort. He always managed to cut an impressive stride and today was no different. Her palms tingled as she remembered the feel of his skin under them.

She hated being distant from Caleb. She hated this huge abyss that had appeared between them—one she didn't know if they'd be able to cross.

Today had felt a little different. Today, he'd taken all the time in the world for them.

When she'd watched him today getting buried in the sand and swimming with the sharks with Tristan it had made her heart melt a little. This was the guy she remembered. He'd been totally focused on making their son happy.

And Tristan had loved being the focus of his father's attention.

Caleb was being easy around her, he was being familiar. He was reminding her of what they used to have. In some ways it was comforting, and in others it hurt because it reminded her of how much they'd lost.

If she ended up on her own this was what she'd miss. This was what her son would miss out on. The real sharing and connection to his father. This was what the new baby would miss too.

By the time she'd paid for the frozen lemonades, Caleb was back, wearing a pair of khaki shorts and a blue polo shirt.

'Better?'

'Much.' He took the lemonade. 'Thanks. Right, where are we headed?'

She pointed to the path reaching out of the resort. 'I thought we could just take a wander along here and see what there is.'

'Fine by me.'

They walked down the long path shaded with palm trees and tropical flowers. As they left the entrance to the resort they passed a few people on bikes. Cars weren't widely used on Bora Bora, and the roads weren't particularly good. There were only a few taxis for the whole island.

They walked towards the main dock of Vaitape. There were a number of shops and cafés dotted along the way. Addison wandered into the first shop they came to.

Across the shelves was a whole variety of wooden carved ornaments of every kind of animal imaginable—plus a few she didn't even recognise.

Hanging from the walls were the colourful *pareo* fabrics worn by the islanders. Every bright colour was there: red, yellow, blue, green and orange. Clothes were nearby with some of the dresses hand-painted with beautiful Tahitian flowers.

Addison picked up a white dress, strapless with a gathered bodice, trimmed with deep pink at the top and around the bottom hem. The skirt of the dress was hand-painted with intricate pale pink flowers and large pale green leaves. Caleb walked up behind her. 'What have you found?'

She held up the dress. 'This. Isn't it gorgeous?'

He held out the skirt. 'Someone painted this?

Really?' His eyes skimmed up and down her body. Unconsciously she found herself sucking in her stomach.

It was ridiculous. She was wearing a long pink jersey beach dress. Nothing was obvious in this. She had no reason to be self-conscious.

'It would suit you—you'd look good in it,' said Caleb decisively. 'Buy it.' He wandered off and picked up some stuffed sharks and stingrays. 'What about these for Tristan?'

She gave a little nod as she still admired the dress. It was madness to buy something like this. She'd never get to wear it back in London—they just wouldn't get the weather. But she really liked it, and the thought of supporting the people on Bora Bora by buying local goods was definitely something she wanted to do.

It only took a few moments to make their purchases and then Addison moved on to the next shop. There she found more jewellery, pendants she could buy for the women who worked with her at the charity. Something simple and easy to carry home.

In the next shop she found black pearl earrings. 'What about these for your secretary?' she asked Caleb.

He raised his eyebrows. 'The secretary that I just deserted for a month without giving her warning?'

Addison tried to think on her toes but she could feel her cheeks start to flush.

He stepped closer. 'What, you told her too? You told Harry and you told Libby, but you didn't tell me?'

She held up her finger. 'I did tell you. I told you weeks before we were going on holiday for a month. *You* chose not to tell me you weren't going to come.'

He could have got angry. He could have got defensive.

Instead, the edges of his lips turned upwards. 'You're just trying to make me look bad,' he quipped.

She walked over to pay for the earrings. 'If the cap fits,' she shot over her shoulder.

He was behind her in an instant, his hands on either side of her hips as she paid. She could feel the whole of his body gently pressed up behind her.

The shop assistant looked up and smiled. 'Honeymoon?' she asked.

'Oh, no.' Addison shook her head and turned to catch the look on Caleb's face. 'That was a long time ago.'

His gaze met hers. And held it.

It seemed like the longest time. It seemed like for ever. The little hairs on her arms stood on end as if a cool breeze had just danced across her skin.

His voice was low. 'Too long,' he whispered.

He threaded his fingers through hers and reached over to take the bag from the shop assistant.

This time as they left Caleb led the way. And he wasn't walking slowly. He was walking quickly and heading straight back to their resort. She almost had to run to keep up. Her heart was racing.

If he undressed her right now, in the bright sunlight, would he notice anything different about her? Of course he would. And it would bring on a whole conversation she didn't know if she was ready for.

Connections had been tenuous these last few days. But at least they were there. And she didn't want to harm that. She wanted to build on them to see if they could recapture some of what had been lost.

As they approached the resort Caleb took a different route. He must have thought it would take them quicker to their bungalow. Instead, it took them on a winding route to a beautiful bandstand covered in pink and red flowers.

'Wow!' Addison's hand shot up to her mouth. Caleb looked from side to side, obviously confused about where they had ended up. 'Where on earth are we?'

She smiled and walked slowly up the steps, setting down her bags. 'It looks like a bandstand. I've no idea why it's at the bottom of the path.' Her hand reached up and touched the dark green foliage. The aroma from the flowers and surrounding plants was intoxicating.

'I can't believe this is here. It's the kind of thing every teenage girl would dream about having in their garden.' She stepped inside. The foliage covered the top of the structure, making it like an enchanted hideaway.

Caleb touched her shoulder. 'I'm almost scared to ask, but what else do teenage girls dream about?' His voice was low and husky.

She sucked in a breath as she turned back towards him. In the shaded bandstand all she could focus on were his brown eyes.

She could feel her heart thudding against her chest and her breath stall somewhere in her throat.

'Addison.' He reached up and tangled his fingers through her hair. She let out a little groan.

He leaned forward a little, blocking out her surrounding view of the tropical flowers. All she could see was Caleb.

But something was different. Something she hadn't seen in such a long time. He had that little twinkle in his eye again. The one that made her think there was no one on this planet like her husband.

His voice was low. 'It seems wrong not to take advantage of such a beautiful setting.'

He bent to kiss her. He tasted of lemonade. His firm lips pressing against hers and gently nudging hers open. One hand stayed in her hair and the other traced light patterns on her back. Everything that he knew she liked.

She couldn't help herself. Her arms lifted automatically and wound around his neck.

Last time they'd been this up close and personal they'd been almost naked. Last time they'd been this close they'd made another baby.

Her body gave an involuntary shudder. Caleb pulled his lips from hers and concentrated on her neck. She could get lost in this. She could get lost in this so easily.

Memories came flooding back. In the first few years all Caleb had done was kiss her. It hadn't mattered where they had been, or what they'd been doing. He'd pulled her into doorways when shopping, and behind trees when they'd been out walking. His hand had permanently been in hers—or his arm had been around her shoulders.

When she'd become pregnant he'd been the most attentive husband on the planet. He'd bought cookery books and tried to master all her favourite recipes. He'd become an expert at running warm bubble baths surrounded by cotton-fresh candles. He'd come with her to every appointment, every scan. He'd huffed and puffed with her through every part of the labour and when Tristan had been born he'd been the proudest father in the world.

He'd spend hours at night sitting looking at their son. Then he'd spend even more time in the small hours of the morning when Tristan had screamed with colic. He'd paced the floor for hours after hours. Addison hadn't been able to bear it. She'd always ended up in tears herself and Caleb had always herded her back to bed.

Even then, even when she'd been tired and exhausted, a kiss from her husband had made everything seem okay.

Why couldn't it do the same now?

Kissing Caleb now was different. It was terrifying. It reminded her of what she could lose. What she would miss.

His kisses moved back up from her neck and around her ear to her lips again. She took a few steps back to the evergreen wall of the bandstand, praying that no one else would choose to walk along this path.

Her hands moved from around his neck,

across his back and under his polo shirt. His warm, firm flesh was under her palms again.

His hand came up and brushed against her breast. She froze. Would he notice? Would he notice her breasts had mysteriously got bigger?

He pulled back for a second. 'Addison?'

Her heart was racing.

'Are you going to tell me what's going on?'

For a second she couldn't breathe. Couldn't move.

It was like a trick question. She wanted to tell him. She wanted to share with him.

But *this* was the Caleb she wanted. Not the one she had back home. The one who had time for her, who had time for Tristan, and would have time for this new baby.

Maybe she was being unrealistic? Maybe she wanted too much? But she'd had it before—and she knew how good they could be together. How good they could be as a family.

She wasn't stupid. Of course life got in the way. Everyone had busy times at work. Other pressures cropped up. She could deal with that. She had dealt with that. The likelihood was that, in seven or eight years' time, they would be permanent chauffeurs for their kids, taking them to football, dance lessons, swimming lessons, music lessons or whatever else they wanted to attend. They'd end up being like ships passing in the night. And she'd cope with that. She would.

But what she needed right now from her husband was that their family had priority. Their family came first. And back home in London? It just wasn't like that. She wanted Caleb back. She wanted her husband back.

'I've missed you,' she whispered.

His brow furrowed. 'But I've been right here.'

She felt tears spring to her eyes. 'But you haven't been. Tristan and I are like parts of your life that don't count any more. I keep thinking it will stop. Work will slow down. But you just take on more and more. Three years, Caleb. That's how long it's been. We never see each other any more, we never spend time together.' She slid her hand out from under his polo shirt.

'I don't want an appointment in your diary. I don't want to speak to your secretary—as much as I love her.'

He waved his hand as he looked at her. 'I'll look at things when I go home. I'll try and pass some things on to Harry. I'll make sure I'm about more.'

Her stomach gave a horrible little twist. He meant it. She knew he meant it.

But he wasn't really getting it. The casual wave of his hand proved that. She wanted to know that she and Tristan were enough for him—were important enough to him to re-evaluate what he was doing.

But her face must have betrayed her. 'What?' he asked. 'What is it? What else is making you so crazy?'

She shook her head and bit her lip.

Caleb dropped his hands and stepped back. 'Tell me, Addison. This is ridiculous. Tell me what else is going on. Because it has to be something. You're making me feel like I'm on trial here—and for what?'

A tear slid down her cheek and she shook her head again. 'I just want to know that you value us. That we're enough to make you stop and think about how you're living your life.'

Now, he was getting frustrated. 'What is this? You gave me an ultimatum and I'm here. I came.'

'You came because you thought you'd still have access to the phone and the Internet. You thought you could still work. Would you have come if you'd known the truth?'

He hesitated. Just for a second. But it was enough.

She threw up her hands. 'See? I'm trying to decide what's best for me, best for Tristan. What use is a husband and father who is never there? Who never connects with his wife or his child?

Who forgets about the things that should be important?'

'What's important? What have I forgot?' Their voices were raised now, ruining the tranquillity of the beautiful gardens.

'You forget everything! I can't rely on you for Tristan.'

'That's not true. I'm Tristan's father. Of course I can be relied upon. And isn't this why we got some extra help?'

She kept her voice steady. 'Lara's not Tristan's parent. Lara is someone we employ. Tell me, Caleb, if I got knocked down by a bus tomorrow is that what you'd do with our son? Have him looked after on a permanent basis while you continued to work ridiculous hours?'

'What a stupid question. Why would you even ask something like that?'

She stared down at her ring. 'Because getting married meant something to me—'

'It meant something to me too!'

She held up her hand and cut him dead. 'This wasn't what I expected. I feel as if I'm a single parent and a single woman. We never see you—you're never around. And even when you do appear you're not with us. Your mind is always on the next business deal.' She took a deep breath. She was exhausted. Emotionally and physically. Being out in the sun all morning, then walking along to the shops, had taken more out of her than she'd thought. Or maybe it was just this—the constant tension in the air between them.

One thing she knew for sure. She didn't want to go back home and for things to continue the way they were.

'You're being ridiculous now. Okay, so I might have been working too much—but that won't be for ever.' Something flickered across his face—as if he'd just realised what she'd said. 'Is that what you want—to be a single woman? Have you met someone else?'

'What? No.' She was horrified he might even suggest that. She'd neither the time nor the inclination to meet anyone else. That was the absolute last thing on her mind. 'All I'm saying is that I can't live the next twenty years like this. In fact, I can't live the next year like this.'

As she said the words something happened. The green around her started to spin.

She heard the shout. 'Addison?' and saw the flash of movement but for a few seconds it was as if she almost weren't there.

She couldn't really focus on anything. She was conscious of being lowered to the floor. It was cool there. It felt fine.

The very next second someone was pinching her hand. 'Addison?'

She blinked but couldn't see him. That was odd.

The face came around from behind her. He was on the floor next to her and she was leaning against his chest.

His hand rubbed up and down her arm, almost as if he was trying to heat her up, but that didn't make sense—because she wasn't cold.

'Addison,' he said again. 'Are you with me?'

She tried to straighten up a little as she looked around. She was on the floor of the bandstand. How on earth did she get there?

His strong arms wrapped around her. 'What happened?'

'You tell me. Do you want me to go and get you a doctor?'

She shook her head quickly. 'No. No doctor. I just felt a bit woozy. We must have been out in the sun too long. Give me a second. I'll be fine.' She pushed herself up onto her knees and sucked in a deep breath to try and clear her head.

She'd been fighting. She'd been fighting with Caleb.

'Are you sick? Are you ill?'

She shook her head again. 'I told you, too much sun.' She stood up and held her hand out to catch hold of the foliage wall. But Caleb was too quick for her, he had his hand in hers and his other arm firmly around her waist.

'Let's get you back to the bungalow. Lie down. I'll get you something to eat and drink. We never had any lunch. Do you think that's what's wrong?'

She tried not to smile. If she counted the days in life she'd missed a meal she'd be here all day. But she'd never done that when she was pregnant. And she'd never done it in a different climate.

'Do you want me to carry you?'

'Don't you dare,' she shot back. 'I'll be fine walking.'

Caleb was still talking. 'I'm still going to ask a doctor to come and see you.'

'No. I don't need a doctor. You're probably right. I probably just need something to eat. I'll be fine.' She glanced at her watch. 'Look at the time. We have to pick up Tristan from the kids' club.'

'Forget the kids' club. He's safe there. Let's get you settled down, then I'll pick up Tristan and take him to play on the beach. That way you get a chance to rest.'

He was steering her along the path, practically doing the walking for her. It only took five minutes to reach the bungalow. He kicked open the beach doors and took her straight inside. The air conditioning was an instant relief. She went to sit down on one of the sofas, then changed her mind.

Caleb was over at the fridge, pulling out a bottle of chilled water. She walked through to the bedroom and pulled off her dress and swimming suit. She wanted room for her body to breathe and the swimming suit felt oddly restrictive.

Even though it was the middle of the day she picked up her short satin nightdress. She was going to lie down for an hour.

'Here you go.' She jumped out of her skin. She was facing the other way and was just dropping the nightdress over her bare behind. She hadn't even thought.

Caleb looked at her as he set the water down next to her bed. 'What's wrong?'

She shook her head. 'Nothing. It's fine. Or I will be once I've had a lie down.'

Her head was spinning. What if she'd been facing the other way? What if he'd noticed her changing figure and actually asked her about it? Could she really have lied to him?

'What about a piece of that chocolate cake you spotted? I could walk over and get you a slice. You could probably do with the sugar boost.'

She sat down on the bed. 'No, maybe tomorrow. I think I'd feel sick if I ate that right now. I'll just have an apple.'

'Nope. Try again. You just keeled over. An apple isn't going to cut it. You need more than that.'

She wrinkled her nose. 'I don't really want anything big.'

He nodded. 'Leave it with me. I'll find something.'

She took a drink of the water and lay back in the comfortable bed. If she could sleep for just an hour she'd be fine. She rested her hand on her stomach. Could she have hurt the baby when she fell? No. Caleb had caught her. There was only a hint of a stomach. But it felt a little firmer.

Maybe her blood pressure had dipped a bit. Or, it was just what she'd thought, she'd skipped a meal and her blood sugar had dipped. That could make anyone woozy.

She closed her eyes for just a second. Only for Caleb to return and shake her shoulder.

'Here, sit up and eat this, then I'll leave you alone.' It was a huge bowl of sliced fruits. Apple, strawberry, melon, grapes, peach and pineapple with some kind of sauce drizzled over it.

'Where did you get this?'

'I spoke nicely to the kitchen. Said you needed something refreshing.' He handed her a fork and sat at the end of the bed.

Now she couldn't hide her amusement. 'What are you doing?'

He folded his arms. 'I'm making sure you eat something.'

'You don't have to watch.'

'Call me a stickler.'

She tasted one of the strawberries. 'Hmm, that's lovely. What's the sauce?'

'I have no idea. Chef's secret.'

She smiled. 'Well, I don't know what it is. But I like it.' She kept eating. He was actually serious. He was going to watch her eat. 'I'm fine. But I'm tired. Once I've eaten this, I'm going to sleep for a while. Why don't you go and get Tristan? We were due to pick him up. I don't want him to think we've forgotten about him.'

Caleb was watching her with those intense brown eyes. He glanced at his watch and sighed. 'You'll eat everything and go for a sleep?'

It was like being told off by the head teacher. But she could actually see the concern on his face. It kind of gave her a warm rush in her stomach. He was actually interested in her. He was actually paying her some attention. How ironic because she needed him to be distracted. She needed him to be thinking about something else.

She gave him a smile. 'Honestly, I'm fine. Thank you. I'll see you and Tristan later.'

She could see him still hesitate. It was hard.

Not long ago they'd been shouting at each other in the bandstand. He'd been angry with her, and she'd been angry with him too.

But as soon as she'd been unwell everything had been forgotten. Caleb had been the model husband. And he still was.

He finally stood up. 'Okay, then.' He picked up the bucket and spade. 'I'll go and get Tristan and take him to the beach.'

He took one step to the door. Then, before she could even think, he crossed the room and dropped a kiss on the top of her head.

'See you later.' He walked out of the door and Addison looked down at the bowl of fruit and held her breath. Once she was sure he was gone she put the bowl down and curled up on the bed.

She pressed her hand to her stomach. 'Stay safe, baby,' she whispered.

Tristan was full of energy. He'd loved playing with the other kids but was even more excited about playing with his dad on the beach.

'Can I bury you again, Daddy?'

Caleb shook his head. 'I don't think you could dig a big enough hole. Let's have a sandcastle competition.'

Tristan agreed and rushed back to the bungalow to find some wrestlers for his castle. He came back thirty seconds later with one for Caleb too.

They played for over an hour. Eventually Tristan flagged. Caleb had set some towels under a few of the palm trees and carried him over to go to sleep.

He could have gone back in the bungalow but didn't want to disturb Addison.

He was horrified by what had happened. A white flash had shot across Addison's face just before her legs had crumpled underneath her. He'd jumped across the bandstand to catch her and lower her to the ground.

Terror. That was what he'd felt. Addison had never had health problems before. She'd always been really healthy. And she'd never talked about fainting before. If he had his way she would have been taken to see the doctor. But she'd insisted she was fine and just needed to lie down.

A horrible feeling of dread crept through him. Some of the things she'd said started to circle around in his mind. Twice. Twice, she'd used the expression 'what if I was hit by a bus?' She'd issued him that ultimatum. Telling him to come on holiday or her and Tristan wouldn't be back.

It didn't matter that the sun was currently splitting the sky, Caleb felt a chill. She was pale, and she'd fainted. She hadn't been eating too much and she hadn't drunk much either—only that strawberry daiquiri the other night.

Was Addison ill? Was something wrong with his wife?

He stood up and started pacing. The more he paced, the more his brain spun around and around. She wanted him to reconnect with her, and reconnect with Tristan. He hadn't even realised they'd disconnected in the first place but he was beginning to realise just how switched off he'd been.

She was definitely acting strangely. And that thing that he couldn't put his finger on was an innate sadness. An aura that had been coming from her since they'd left on holiday.

He could feel himself start to panic—something Caleb definitely wasn't used to. Could Addison really be ill?

But she'd tell him—wouldn't she? His breath caught in his throat. That was what she'd been telling him. That was what she'd been spelling out. He was never there to tell. How could she tell him if there was actually something wrong with her if he was never there to have that conversation?

He couldn't bear it. He couldn't bear it if his beautiful wife was ill. He looked around him. His heart skipped a beat. Paradise. She'd booked them a month in paradise.

Was there more to this? Was Addison more than ill? His hand reached out to the nearest palm tree. He squeezed his eyes closed. Her sister had died of cancer. She'd spoken before about being worried it was in her genes.

Was that why she kept giving him a scenario where she wasn't around?

He knelt to the ground and put his hands on his head. Tristan was sleeping peacefully at his feet. Was there a chance his son might not have a mother in the future?

He felt sick. He felt physically sick.

Was she trying to give them this time to create some more memories together? Was she hoping he might form a better connection to Tristan in case she wasn't there in the future?

This was all crazy. It was all in his head. But what if there were a tiny possibility any of it could be true?

He groaned. He'd shouted at her. For the first time in his life he'd actually shouted at her.

When he'd kissed her, he'd thought things might start to get back on track for them. He'd always loved kissing Addison and today had been no different. He loved the smell of her hair, the touch of her skin. He loved the shade of lipstick she liked to wear, and how she had to fold her clothes a certain way.

He loved the fact when she was reading a

book she always put it down with the back facing upwards, like a warning not to touch. He loved the fact she would happily buy a box of chocolates, eat the orange and strawberry creams and leave the rest.

He loved the fact that when they had guests around to dinner, she'd frequently run along the street to the local Belgian patisserie and buy a giant pavlova, decorate it with fruit and pretend she'd made it.

He let out a long, slow breath. All these little things. All these little things that they'd both forgotten about over the last few years. He hadn't really had time to think about.

She was right. She was right about everything.

They'd been drifting apart from each other and he hadn't even noticed.

He hadn't paid her and Tristan the attention that they deserved. He hadn't been around them enough.

And when she'd actually tried to talk to him—or he'd tried to talk to her—both had made some kind of excuse not to have that conversation. It was almost as if they'd forgotten how to communicate with each other.

He hadn't wanted to listen. He didn't want to acknowledge his part in all this. He just wanted to pretend that everything was fine. That nothing had gone wrong between them.

Was he actually in danger of losing so much more than he could even imagine?

Addison had to be here. She had to be in his life. He couldn't function without her. She was the glue that held him together.

When she'd fainted today he'd been shocked. She looked so pale and so fragile. Was she afraid if he called a doctor to see her, he might find out something she didn't want him to know?

He had to try and temper his feelings and emotions. He had to respect Addison's wishes. She'd said no and if he went over her head and asked Reception to call a doctor it would cause yet another fight between them that they didn't need.

He picked up the sleeping Tristan and walked as silently as possible into the bungalow, putting Tristan in his own bed. Then, he walked quickly back over to the reception area and into the resort shop. It only took him a few minutes to find what he was looking for.

He was determined to make things right. He was determined to make things better.

He was doing his best to push all the other stuff out of his mind. The fact that there might actually be something wrong with his wife.

He had to concentrate on the here and now.

And that was him and Addison. Him, Addison and Tristan.

Hopefully, by the time she woke, he would have started to build bridges between them. He needed his wife to have faith in him. He needed his wife to trust him enough to tell him what was on her mind.

And he had to start somewhere.

# FREE Merchandise is 'in the Cards' for you!

Dear Reader,

## *We're giving away FREE MERCHANDISE!*

Seriously, we'd like to reward you for reading this novel by giving you **FREE MERCHANDISE** worth over $20 retail. And no purchase is necessary!

You see the Jack of Hearts sticker above? Paste that sticker in the box on the Free Merchandise Voucher inside. Return the Voucher promptly...and we'll send you valuable Free Merchandise!

Thanks again for reading one of our novels—and enjoy your Free Merchandise with our compliments!

*Pam Powers*

Pam Powers

P.S. Look inside to see what Free Merchandise is **"in the cards"** for you!

# W

e'd like to send you two free books like the one you are enjoying now. Your two books have a combined price of over $10 retail, but they are yours to keep absolutely FREE! We'll even send you 2 wonderful surprise gifts. You can't lose!

**HARLEQUIN**

*Romance*

*Pregnant with a Royal Baby!*

THE PRINCES OF XAVIERA

**Susan Meier**

**HARLEQUIN**

*Romance*

*Swept into the Rich Man's World*

**Katrina Cudmore**

**REMEMBER:** Your Free Merchandise, consisting of **2 Free Books** and **2 Free Gifts**, is worth over $20 retail! No purchase is necessary, so please send for your Free Merchandise today.

# YOUR FREE MERCHANDISE INCLUDES...

2 FREE Books **AND** 2 FREE Mystery Gifts

## FREE MERCHANDISE VOUCHER

2 FREE
BOOKS
and
2 FREE
GIFTS

Please send my Free Merchandise, consisting of
**2 Free Books** and **2 Free Mystery Gifts**.
I understand that I am under no obligation to buy
anything, as explained on the back of this card.

### 119/319 HDL GKAR

*Please Print*

|  |
|---|

FIRST NAME

|  |
|---|

LAST NAME

|  |
|---|

ADDRESS

| | |
|---|---|

APT.#          CITY

| | |
|---|---|

STATE/PROV.          ZIP/POSTAL CODE

## NO PURCHASE NECESSARY!

HR-516-FMH16

◄ If offer card is missing write to: Reader Service, P.O. Box 1867, Buffalo, NY 14240-1867 or visit www.ReaderService.com ◄

**BUSINESS REPLY MAIL**
FIRST-CLASS MAIL    PERMIT NO. 717    BUFFALO, NY

POSTAGE WILL BE PAID BY ADDRESSEE

**READER SERVICE**
PO BOX 1867
BUFFALO NY 14240-9952

NO POSTAGE
NECESSARY
IF MAILED
IN THE
UNITED STATES

# CHAPTER FIVE

WHEN SHE FINALLY woke someone had drawn the shutters on the beach bungalow's windows. Even though they blocked out the sun, the wind was still able to get through them and, as the window was open, the full-length white curtain was fluttering in the wind. Just how long had she been asleep?

She stretched and sat up, taking a little drink of the now lukewarm water. She glanced at the clock. Nearly two hours. That was how long she'd slept. But the surprising thing was, she really did feel better for it.

Something caught her eye. A flickering. She stood up and took a few steps forward, stopping at the entrance to the large en suite bathroom and catching her breath.

The lights were out in the bathroom and it was lit only by an array of candles around the edges of the white bath. The bath was full with bubbles reaching right to the top, the aroma of vanilla, frangipani and orange pulling her in.

She couldn't help but smile. Caleb. Caleb had done this for her. There was even a little dish with some dark chocolates in it and a glass of white wine sitting next to the bath. She walked over and touched the side of the glass. Condensation wet her finger; it must have only been poured recently.

Where did he get all this? Had he gone shopping while she'd been sleeping?

She heard some shouts outside and walked through to the main room. The doors were wide open to the beach. Caleb and Tristan were running in and out of the surf and from the variety of characters spread at the entrance it was obvious she'd just missed a wrestling match.

This was the kind of thing she'd dreamt of. When she'd sat in the travel agency and made the booking, this was the kind of thing she'd wished for their family holiday. Caleb and Tristan were happy. At first he'd looked a little awkward—as if he were having trouble actually relaxing—but now they were playing just the way a father and son should.

She walked back through to the bathroom and pulled her nightdress over her head. What about the wine? She couldn't drink it, so she poured a little of it down the toilet. He would never know.

The bath was perfect. She tied her hair up in a knot and sank down into the bubbles. Part of her was grateful and part of her felt a little guilty—because she knew that was how Caleb was feeling.

That was why he'd done this. He'd obviously got a fright this afternoon and so had she.

It was clear their fight was never going to be mentioned again. But how did they move on from here?

She wanted to hope that things were going to change. She wanted to hope things were going to be better. But she didn't want that to be because she was pregnant. It had to be because Caleb had realised that things had reached breaking point and had to turn around.

When they'd been fighting earlier he couldn't even acknowledge what was wrong. Had her being unwell been his wake-up call?

The little seeds of thought that had planted in her brain earlier started to sprout tiny shoots and grow. Maybe this wasn't all Caleb's fault? Maybe she should shoulder some of the responsibility too?

They'd argued about having more kids. She'd just assumed he would agree. Instead, he'd drawn further away and she'd felt more and more isolated.

The atmosphere in the house had changed.

And part of that was her. She definitely felt a little hostile towards him. Why didn't he want to expand their family?

She closed her eyes and rested her hand on her stomach. She was praying for so much right now. She was praying for this baby, praying for her marriage and praying for herself. She hadn't just struggled when Tristan had been born.

She'd felt numb. It had been as if everything was happening around her. Even now she struggled to put it into words. She hadn't felt that initial wave of love that others talked about. She'd felt relief that labour was finally over. Then, when everyone else had left, she'd stared at the little baby in the crib and wondered how on earth she would love him as she was supposed to.

Now, she knew that love was something that grew and embedded itself into you every single day. For a while she'd felt disjointed. And the numbness had spread to her relationship with Caleb. Was she failing everybody?

But gradually things had changed. The terrifying screaming bundle had become manageable. Tristan eventually learned to sleep for more than ten minutes at a time. The ache and constant mastitis in her breasts—the thing that made breastfeeding excruciating—finally quietened down. Her health visitor persuaded her to let Caleb bottle feed Tristan with expressed breastmilk for a few hours every night. At first the guilt had crippled her. She was failing at feeding her child too. But gradually she learned to relax about it. He was gaining weight. He was thriving. The mastitis was settling. She felt more rested. Now, she could feed him during the day and early evening without associating it with pain and discomfort. And Tristan started to react to her. He smiled. He watched her. He giggled. And the connection between them grew, just like the connection between her and Caleb.

This was why she was determined to be prepared this time around. Maybe this was why she was reluctant to tell him? Was there a chance that Caleb might not be happy about her being pregnant again? This baby hadn't been planned. And now, there could be other difficulties.

But it was the oddest feeling. Her hand pressed against her stomach. Even with all the issues, she was happy that their baby was in place. She could feel a surge of love. There was no numbness. This baby was loved already.

The warm water was relaxing her muscles and letting all the tension dissolve away. Wine would have been perfect. Chocolate would just have to do.

It was the little things. The little things that

showed he was considering her again. She just had to see where that would take them.

Addison finally appeared at the doorway a few hours later. Caleb had just thrown Tristan over his shoulder for the last time.

'Hey, how are you feeling?' The empty wine glass was in her hands.

'Good. Thank you. The bath was great.' She did look better. There was a little more colour in her cheeks and she'd changed into a bright green short dress scattered with tiny sequins.

'How about we take it easy tonight too? Do you want to order room service?'

Tristan wriggled around in his dad's arms. 'We're going in the shower. And then I'm getting some sausages.' He pointed over at the bungalow on the water. 'Can we all sleep in there tonight? We haven't yet and I want to watch the fishes.'

Caleb shrugged. He didn't want to do anything that would tax her, but room service and crossing the walkway to the water bungalow should be fine. 'What do you think? We could all just sleep in the big bed?'

She hesitated. 'What if Tristan wakes up in the night and wanders out? I'd hate for anything to happen.'

Caleb nodded. 'Let me check. Although we

haven't been using our locks much around here, I'm sure there is a lock on the bungalow door. We could lock it for through the night and that way we know he's safe with us.'

She gave a little smile. 'Yeah, that sounds good. It might be nice to listen to the sea while we're in bed.'

'Right, then, I'm going to throw us in the shower and we'll be back to order dinner soon.'

Half an hour later they were sitting at the table in the over-water bungalow eating dinner. They'd both gone for the speciality fish of the day—red tuna—and Tristan was happy with his sausages, potatoes and peas. There were a few other families on the beach and the staff came out and set up the screen for the film.

'What is it tonight?' asked Addison. 'Do you know?'

He gave a little laugh. 'I think it's *Jaws*.'

Her mouth fell open. 'It is not. No way. They can't show that on an island where sharks are around every day.'

He smiled. 'Okay, maybe it's not. I think it's a comedy about weddings.'

She flung her napkin at him. 'Rat fink.' She shook her head. 'I love those kinds of films, but I'm just too tired. Do you mind missing it?'

'Of course not. Anyway, I've moved things

around a little inside. We won't need to watch a film.'

Tristan was looking very pleased with himself. 'I helped Daddy.' He looked over his shoulder. 'But don't tell anyone we've done it.'

Now, she was definitely curious. She hadn't been back inside the over-water bungalow lately. 'What on earth have you two done?'

Caleb and Tristan bumped elbows and gave each other conspiratorial glances. 'Let's wait until after dinner,' said Caleb. 'We'll keep it as a surprise.'

Addison gave a nod. It was so nice seeing them like this. There was no getting away from the fact that, like a lot of little boys, Tristan hero-worshipped his dad. Had she got in the way of that? She'd stopped trying to organise time for them both together. She'd used to attend a yoga class once a week and they'd always had some time alone then. But after missing a few classes she'd stopped making the effort and the time for the two of them had been lost.

Now, Tristan was in his element as he had his father's full attention. Which was exactly how it should be.

Caleb stretched his hand across the table and gave her hand a squeeze. 'You feeling okay?'

'I'm good. I don't know what happened earlier. Maybe it was the heat? Or maybe it was something I ate.'

His face was shaded from the sun lowering in the sky, but it couldn't hide his intense brown eyes that were fixed on her. She was trying to deflect—and he wasn't buying it for a second.

He hadn't moved his hand. It stayed exactly where it was. 'You won't let me get you checked over by a doctor?'

She shook her head. That was the last thing she wanted. She knew exactly what was wrong with her—she just wasn't ready to share. But the fact that she could see on his face that he was truly worried about her gave her a warm little glow.

At first she'd been so mixed up, so confused. She'd needed time to process what Dr Mackay had told her. And none of her initial decisions had changed but she was gradually becoming calmer.

If her baby had Down's syndrome she would cope. She'd been given an early warning. She would have time to prepare. Time to speak to Dr Mackay at length and have her other scans carried out. If there were heart issues, hearing or vision problems, then she'd have to prepare herself for what lay ahead.

One thing was for certain. She already loved

this child. It was part of Caleb and it was part of her.

She put her best smile on her face. 'I don't need to be checked over. I'm fine.'

He slowly pulled his hand away. 'I've changed our booking for the snorkelling. It was supposed to be tomorrow but I thought we could delay it for a few days. Just until you're sure everything's fine.'

He was being cautious. He was being careful with her.

'We'll just have a day on the beach tomorrow, or around the pool. Tristan can jump around in the kids' club for a while and I'll entertain him for the rest of the day. You could go to the resort spa if you wanted to.'

What a nice thought. On a regular day she'd love a massage or manicure. But after the day she'd had she wasn't ready for anything like that. And she wasn't entirely sure if some of the massage oils were suitable for use in pregnancy. This was a small place. If she asked the question word could get out.

She shook her head. 'Not tomorrow. But maybe next week. A day at the pool sounds good. You know what? I might even make you buy me a piece of that chocolate cake.'

He gave her a careful nod. It was obvious he

was prepared to give her a little leeway right now. And she'd take it.

She was beginning to see flashes of the Caleb that she'd fallen in love with again. It was reminding her of exactly what could lie ahead.

He was attentive again. He was talking to her, *really* talking to her, without having a hundred business deals in his head. He was looking at her again as if she actually existed, instead of just being part of the furniture.

Things were moving in the right direction.

But was this a permanent change or just a temporary holiday arrangement?

Addison's face was a picture. 'How on earth did you do this?'

He and Tristan exchanged proud looks. They'd rearranged the whole over-water bungalow. The key feature in the bungalow was the glass panel, normally housed beneath the coffee table, which showed the underwater activity in the coral beneath the bungalow. Tristan loved it. And Caleb loved it too. He'd never seen fish like it. Every colour under the rainbow, some darting past, some spending hours around the coral.

So, he'd managed to upend the giant bed onto its side and push it through from the bedroom into the living room. Then he'd dragged the sofa back through to the other room. Now, they could lie in bed tonight and watch the fish swim right in front of them.

Addison raised her eyebrows. 'Do you think we'll get in trouble?'

He winked. 'I won't tell if you won't.'

She held out her hand to Tristan. 'Want to go and get ready for bed, buster?'

He jumped up and down. 'I'm going to watch the fishes all night!'

It didn't take long for them to get ready. They changed for bed, closed up the beach bungalow and took along a few snacks. Caleb held up the bottle of wine he'd grabbed from the fridge. 'Want a glass of wine?'

Addison glanced at Tristan. 'No, not tonight. I'll just have some water.' She walked over and plucked the giant bag of crisps from his hand. 'But I might take charge of these. I don't want crumbs in the bed.'

It didn't take them long to be tucked up in the giant bed. They locked the main door but left the curtains open so they could watch the spectacular sunset, shooting reds and oranges across the darkening sky.

Tristan shouted every time he saw a new fish. By the time his eyelids were starting to droop he'd given them all names. He crawled back up into the middle of the bed and zonked out.

Addison was lying facing Caleb, Tristan's head between them.

'What do we do now?' she teased. Her blonde hair had fallen over her face and her bare shoulder was revealed with only the tiny spaghetti strap of her satin nightie showing.

He groaned. 'Don't even go there. We're stuck—locked in our water bungalow—with a sleeping four-year-old between us.' He lifted up his hands and laughed. 'I couldn't make this up if I tried.'

The last rays of the sun were illuminating the dark sky behind her. For once the shadows were gone from her eyes. She didn't look tired. She just looked relaxed.

'I'm sorry I haven't been around,' he whispered.

She licked her lips. 'Sorry can be easy to say, Caleb. What happens when we get home?'

There was a little flutter inside his chest. 'I wasn't sure you were coming home.'

'Neither was I.' She gave her head the slightest shake. 'I need to be sure.'

'Sure about what? Sure that I love you? Of course I do. I always have. I always will.'

Her eyes filled up.

'Addison, tell me what's going on.' He kept the frustration out of his voice. He kept his tone neutral.

Her jaw tightened. Seconds before she'd been happy. Seconds before she'd been relaxed. Why had he even started this? He should have left her alone. He should have been happy that they'd all ended up in bed together as a family. After the day she'd had, it should have been enough.

She lifted her hands. '*This* is what's going on. Us.'

He felt every muscle in his body tighten. He wasn't going to get angry. He wasn't. No matter how frustrated he felt.

Instead he stroked his finger down her arm. Lightly. Gently. None of the things that he felt right now, but everything he had to show his wife.

When he reached her hand, he slid his palm over her hand and intertwined their fingers. 'This is us,' he whispered. 'This is exactly us.'

A tear escaped down her cheek. 'I hope so,' she whispered before she closed her eyes and went to sleep.

# CHAPTER SIX

CALEB HAD BEEN tiptoeing around her for the last three days. They'd virtually done nothing apart from eat food, take Tristan to kids' club for a few hours, walk around the resort and relax in the shade.

She'd finished three books. If she kept going like this she'd have to wander around the pool and steal someone else's book while they were in swimming.

They'd slept in the over-water bungalow for two nights and then eventually gone back to the beach bungalow after Tristan had tried sleeping like a starfish. Tristan had slept in his own room and Caleb had cuddled in behind her with his arms around her.

When they walked around the resort he held her hand or had his arm around her shoulder.

The waiter arrived with breakfast as usual. Because she felt so rested she'd been up early this morning and was ravenous. Caleb had gone for a run along the beach and came back with the sweat dripping from him.

He emerged from the shower towelling his hair and grinned at her heaped plate of scrambled eggs with toast. Tristan was lining up all his sausages in a row to match his toast soldiers. 'Is there anything left?'

She shook her head. 'We decided to put you on a diet. Coffee only.'

He laughed and poured himself a cup before finding his breakfast hidden under a silver dome. 'Better eat up quickly, Tristan, we're going snorkelling this morning.'

Tristan's eyes lit up. 'Snorkelling? Yeah! Will we find Nemo?'

Caleb gave her a little wink. 'I have it on good authority that there definitely should be a whole school of Nemos where we're going.'

Tristan opened the picture book they'd bought him of all the different fish around the island. He pointed to the bright orange and white clown fish. 'That's Nemo,' he said seriously to Addison. 'That's the one I'm looking for.'

'Doesn't he sometimes hide in the sea anemones?'

Tristan looked over his shoulder. 'Only if a barracuda is about. They can be very bad.'

Addison nodded. He was so serious. He was going to love today.

She flung some things together into a bag.

Caleb appeared behind her. 'Are you sure you're okay with this? You don't need to come if you don't want to.'

She grabbed her floppy hat. 'It's only two hours and it's quite close by. I think it'll be fine. If I don't feel well, I'll let you know.'

There were eight other people waiting to board the white boat to the nearby coral reef. They were a happy bunch, all clutching onto small snorkels and goggles. The journey across the lagoon to one of the small atolls only took five minutes. Once they arrived they had the option of joining the snorkelling or staying on the nearby beach.

Addison had dressed carefully. She was wearing a swimming costume, black with white panels at the side, which gave the illusion that her waist hadn't thickened quite as much as it had. She wouldn't slip her dress off until the last minute, and hopefully, since she'd be in waist-high water, nothing would be noticed.

Tristan was jumping around. He was wearing an all-in-one, which meant she didn't need to put quite so much sunscreen on as before.

As soon as they arrived, Caleb jumped into the water with the rest of the adults and held his hands out for Tristan. Perfect. It gave her time to get into the water unobserved.

The coral was beautiful. Jaggy in places, but the boat crew gave them some plastic shoes for their feet.

All the tourists spread out amongst the coral reef, keeping relatively still so as not to scare any marine life away. But there was no need to worry—the marine life was abundant.

It took Tristan a few goes to get the hang of using the snorkel. Once he'd figured out he could breathe with his head under the water he loved it.

Addison had lowered herself into the water as Caleb taught Tristan how to use his snorkel. By the time she reached them they were in slightly deeper water with it almost reaching their shoulders.

'Hey, guys, this is great.'

Caleb reached out and hugged her with his spare arm. He was holding onto Tristan with the other.

Tristan's head bobbed back up. 'I think I've just seen Nemo!' he exclaimed.

They all put their heads back under just in time to see a cluster of orange and white clown fish dart around the coral reef. Addison had her camera and took a quick snap.

It seemed that Tristan had memorised the whole book of tropical reef fish. He could name just about all of them. By the time they'd finished he'd spotted blue and yellow scribbled angel fish, orange spiny squirrel fish, blue and orange majestic angelfish and yellow trumpet fish. Addison snapped as many pictures as she could.

It was easy. It was relaxing. At one point Caleb grabbed her around the waist and planted a kiss on her lips, then laughed at her shocked expression. 'Last time I kissed you, you fainted. I thought at least if I kissed you in water it might break your fall.' He leaned forward and pressed his forehead against hers. 'It seems I make women weak at the knees.'

She thudded her hand off his chest. 'And I was just trying to improve your reflexes. It's said they get slower with age. What age are you next birthday?'

This was what they used to be like. Teasing each other constantly. And she'd missed that. More than she'd even realised.

The guide shouted everyone back to the boat. Addison had a mild moment of panic that she'd be right next to Caleb and he might notice her changing figure. She needed to tell him. And she needed to tell him soon.

But as they moved towards the boat the other tourists separated them. She was able to climb back on board and slip her dress over her head before reaching down to grab Tristan.

The journey back was quick and after a shower they dropped Tristan off at kids' club for a few hours.

'What do you want to do today?' asked Caleb.

He looked totally chilled, totally relaxed. He was strolling along in a pair of knee-length khaki shorts and a short-sleeved white shirt, with his hair still damp from the shower. His skin was starting to turn a golden brown colour—the shade that her paler skin would never reach. It made him suit his white shirt all the more and she could see the admiring glances from some other passers-by. She couldn't resist teasing him some more.

She turned towards him. 'I think I want to be bad.'

He almost tripped over his own feet. His hands shot out from his pockets. 'What?'

She stepped right up in front of him, momentarily sucking her stomach in, and pressing her body against his. As soon as she moved the telltale gleam appeared in his eyes.

She ran one finger up from his waist to his chest. 'I think I want some chocolate cake.' She stepped back and laughed.

He shook his head and started laughing too. He stuck his hands back in his pockets and walked past her. 'Just for that,' he growled playfully over his shoulder, 'there'll be no chocolate cake for you.'

She kept laughing and ran to catch up with him, tucking her arm in his as they walked to the patisserie.

'Coffee?' he asked as he grabbed a tray.

She shook her head. 'No, decaf tea for me.'

He bent down and glanced behind her.

'What are you doing?'

He stood back up. 'Who are you and what have you done with my coffee-addicted wife?'

She shrugged. 'I fancied a change.'

'Just as long as that's all you're changing,' he shot back as he placed their order.

Her stomach gave a little flip-flop. He was joking. She knew he was. But she also realised how her actions were affecting him. He might look relaxed and chilled, but things were obviously still preying on his mind as much as they were hers.

She'd seen the change in him. She'd seen the improvement. She finally felt as if she was re-capturing a little of what they'd lost. She just needed to know it would continue when they got back home. It was amazing how different he could be when he wasn't permanently at-tached to his work.

They sat down at a shaded table next to the

lagoon. One of the resort staff was putting leaf-lets on all the tables.

Addison picked one up.

'What is it?' asked Caleb as he set down the cakes and drinks.

She turned it around to face him. 'It's a ball at the resort next door. Apparently they do it every year to support breast cancer.'

He gave her a smile. 'Did they know you were coming? You won't be able to resist something like that.'

He reached over to read the leaflet. 'What do you think?'

He was right. She couldn't usually resist a chance to support a fellow cancer charity. 'I didn't exactly bring any clothes suitable for a ball. And I'm quite sure you didn't either.'

He gave a nod. 'You could be right. I think I'm going to run out of socks before we get home.'

'And I'm quite sure they won't allow kids at a ball. Isn't the resort next door for adults only?'

He nodded. 'Yeah. I hadn't thought about that. But they do have a babysitting service here. If it was someone we trusted—like the girls from the kids' club—maybe we could arrange that?'

Addison took her first bite of the chocolate cake. Wow. She sagged back into her seat.

Caleb raised his eyebrows. 'That good?'

She nodded and his fork was over in an instant, swiping a piece of her cake. 'Hey!'

He put it in his mouth quickly and she watched his face. When the taste hit he sagged back in his chair too. 'Oh,' was all he said.

'Yip, oh.'

He gave her a cheeky wink and lifted up his lemon tart. 'How about a swap?'

She picked up her plate and held it close to her chest. 'Not a chance. Get your own.'

He put down his own fork and pushed his plate away. 'Nope. Can't eat that now. It's a poor second place. I'll make do with the coffee.'

She grinned at him. 'I hope you aren't trying to guilt me into sharing.'

He shook his head. 'I know you too well for that.'

One of the staff walked past and paused when she saw his plate. 'You didn't like the lemon tart?'

He hesitated. Obviously a bit embarrassed. He hadn't even had a chance to reply before the ever-efficient member of staff picked up the plate. 'Shall I swap it for something else?'

She was facing Caleb and had her back to Addison.

She scowled at him and mouthed *don't you dare*. But he shot the woman a beaming smile and nodded, pointing at Addison's plate. 'Could

I have a piece of the chocolate cake the same as my wife, please?'

She gave a nod and hurried off.

Addison leaned across the table towards him. 'I can't believe you got away with that.'

He laughed. 'Neither can I.'

The staff member brought the cake back and nodded to the leaflet on their table. 'Oh, the ball. It's fabulous. We wouldn't normally publicise an event at another resort, but this one is special and it is for charity. Are you going to go?'

Addison smiled. 'We'd love to, but we didn't exactly bring any clothes suitable to wear to a ball—' she pointed towards Caleb's shorts and her sundress '—and we'd need to find a babysitter for our son.'

Caleb gave her a quick wink and pulled the chocolate cake towards him, taking his first forkful.

The staff member waved her hand. 'Oh, don't worry about clothes. Most people don't bring anything special. We have somewhere you can hire clothes. There are dresses suitable for a ball—' she turned towards Caleb, whose mouth was currently full of chocolate cake '—and suits for the gentlemen. And we have a babysitter service at the resort. It comes highly recommended. You can even request which sitter you get.'

# CHAPTER SEVEN

HE WAS STILL nuzzling at her neck an hour later.
'What time is it?'

'Time we picked up our son.'

They'd just about made it back inside. She
dreaded to think what items of clothing might
have fluttered past others on an ocean breeze.

If he'd noticed any change in her figure he
hadn't mentioned it but, the truth was, she might
have distracted him.

'Please tell me tonight's film is suitable view-
ing for a kid,' he mumbled.

They were lucky. It was. They sat on the beach
with Tristan sitting at their feet. He watched part
of the old Hollywood musical that was showing, then proceeded to play with his wrestlers.

She was lucky too. It was the same waiter that
served them and as he bent to ask her what she
wanted, he gave her an unobtrusive wink and
asked, 'No mint?'

She gave a nod and when the drink arrived she could tell it was alcohol free. Perfect.

Except it wasn't perfect. She wanted to be honest with her husband. She wanted to tell him the truth. But he'd been trying so hard these last few days. They were recapturing everything she wanted to and there was no mistaking that the little part inside that she'd thought had died or gone numb was very much alive. Every day she fell a little in love with her husband again.

She was afraid that when she told him the truth they'd be plummeted back to reality. Back to the fact that this baby could be at risk. Back to getting their heads around the real world, the plans they might need to make and consider.

Before, she'd just been angry. Angry that this had happened to her and angry that she couldn't share with her husband because he was never around.

Leaving and doing this on her own had actually seemed like the simplest option.

But that was because she wasn't allowing her heart to enter the equation. Practicalities could be so much simpler. But practicalities came without the emotional support that every person needed.

What she needed was the husband she had beside her right now. The husband that was caring, attentive and obviously loved his family.

Could they just stay here for ever, trapped in this little bubble?

She sighed and put her head down onto her knees. Even her daydreams were stupid. A place with no phone or Internet wouldn't be any use. She didn't even know what kind of medical facilities they had on the island.

His work wasn't here and her charity wasn't here. No. Her brain wasn't even going to allow her to have that daydream for a few seconds.

She put her head up just in time to see the hero and heroine of the musical dancing in each other's arms. They were quietly singing to each other.

Her heart gave a little squeeze. It was clear from the heroine's expression on her face she was wishing for something she couldn't have. Was that what she was doing too?

She picked up her drink and took a quick sip to ease her dry throat. She didn't really want that to happen to her. She wanted to have this baby. She wanted her husband by her side, loving this baby just as much as she did. She wanted Tristan to love his baby brother or sister.

Caleb chose that moment to slide his hand up her back. 'Hey, what's wrong?'

He glanced at the screen and smiled. 'Wanna dance? Want me to sing to you?'

She laughed. 'Please no. No one deserves

that.' She shifted position and let her head fall on his shoulder.

Soon. She'd tell him soon.

# CHAPTER EIGHT

'How are you feeling?'

He'd made plans for them today but wanted to make sure Addison was fit enough.

She leaned up in the bed and rested her head on her hand. The smallest action and it gave him a little pang. When they'd first married Addison's still-sleepy face had been his favourite sight first thing in the morning. These days he always left before her alarm had even sounded. He missed that look.

'I'm fine. What's up?'

He moved over and sat at the side of the bed. 'I'd made plans for us to take a tour of the island today.'

'On a boat again?'

'No. On that single track they call a road,' he joked. 'Apparently they take us in a four-by-four. It takes us part way up the mountain, around the lagoon and, if you want, we can take a little walk into the jungle. But if you don't feel up to it, it's fine. I can cancel.'

She shook her head and sat up in the bed. 'I told you, I'm fine. Too much sun and too little food—that's all it was. What time do we go?'

He smiled. She wanted to go. She even seemed pleased. Little by little it felt as if they were reconnecting again. She didn't seem quite so angry any more. Every day she was a little more relaxed. A little more open to his touches and gestures.

'In around an hour. We have plenty of time for breakfast.'

She drank tea again. It was becoming a habit. He could hardly believe she'd stopped drinking coffee. But at least she ate some breakfast: some eggs and a croissant with butter and jam.

An hour later they were ready to go. Addison had her floppy hat with light baggy trousers and a green strappy top. Her sunglasses were already on her face and she'd covered them all in suncream. Tristan had insisted on bringing a wrestler with him and they all bought bottles of water before they left the resort.

As they waited outside Reception an older-style four-by-four screeched up next to them and their exuberant guide jumped out. 'Connor family? Welcome to the land tour of Bora Bora!'

Addison raised her eyebrow at Caleb and grabbed hold of Tristan's hand. 'Yes, that's us.'

'I'm Hiro, your guide. Jump on, folks, you're going to have the time of your lives!'

Caleb helped Tristan and Addison up into the four-by-four and gave Hiro a nod as he climbed on board. He'd barely sat down before the Jeep took off again. They picked up another couple at the next resort then Hiro gave them some maps for their tour.

'We have lots in store today. We'll meet another two cars on the way. We'll head up the mountain first to catch some spectacular views, then we'll take a tour of some World War II relics left on the island and some ancient religious sites. We also plan a little tour into the jungle to show off some of the island's natural fauna. If anyone has anywhere particular they want to go, let us know. We're flexible.'

Addison smiled and sat back in her seat. Caleb double-checked Tristan's seat belt and held onto the handle on the door. 'Watch out for the bumpy roads,' shouted Hiro as they took off again.

'They're not kidding,' said Addison under her breath as they bumped along. The resort staff had already told them that the road around the lagoon and the few inland roads had been cut out by the US military during World War II to allow the transportation of cannons and ammunition.

The journey part way up Mount Otemanu was entertaining. Hiro pointed up above them. 'Our beautiful lady is believed to have been formed from two volcanoes that rose from the ocean floor seven million years ago. She is mainly unspoilt.' They stopped part way up the mountain and Hiro turned his attention to Tristan.

'I have a little story for you, young man.'

Tristan's eyes widened. It was clear he was mesmerised by their cheerful guide. Hiro reached over and picked Tristan up, turning him around to look up at the green-covered peak. 'Look closely. Do you see that cave, halfway up the mountain?'

They all followed his gaze. Sure enough, a gap in the greenery revealed a cave in the side of the mountain. 'It's a very special cave,' he said proudly. 'It's called Te Ana Opea. Some people call it the clinging cave.' He moved his face closer to Tristan's. 'I'll tell you a secret,' he said in a pretend whisper.

'What?' Tristan's eyes were still wide.

Hiro was delighted with his audience. The man was a true performer. 'There's a legend in Bora Bora that a couple who stayed in the cave had a child with the body of a human and a head...' he paused, building excitement '...of a centipede!'

Tristan gasped and put his hand over his mouth. 'Can I see it? Can I see it?'

Hiro, the storyteller, lowered his voice again. 'No one has ever seen it. But the centipede's name was Veri and legend has it that every night the terrifying screams of a child can be heard coming from the cave.'

Caleb shot a look at Addison. Would she be annoyed that Hiro was going to give their child nightmares? But she was taking it in the humour it was given. She was shaking her head and smiling. Tristan started to smile too.

He pushed Hiro's shoulder. 'You're kidding.'

Hiro shrugged. 'Just listen tonight. See if you can hear anything.'

They stopped a little further down the mountain where there was a gap and Hiro pointed out the panoramic view of several privately owned *motu*s. Several belonged to long-standing island families but others were owned by billionaires and rock stars.

Addison turned to Caleb and gave him a nudge. 'Buy me a *motu*, Caleb. I want my own little island, palm trees, white beach and clear blue water all around.'

Hiro laughed. 'For the smallest *motu*, it costs around a million dollars. Good luck, my friend.'

Caleb slung his arm around Addison's shoulders. 'Sorry, honey, I guess you're going to have to make do with a rock—or maybe even a boulder.'

Hiro winked at him. 'We can help you out with something else a little later.'

The Jeep started again and Addison frowned. 'What on earth is he talking about?'

Caleb shook his head. 'I have no idea. Maybe I should get worried.'

Next stop was at the edge of the jungle. Hiro handed out hats to the guests who didn't have one. 'You need one to keep the bugs off,' he said.

Caleb dug into his pocket and pulled out Tristan's baseball cap with the flap at the back for his neck. Addison already had her hat and he smiled at the one Hiro handed to him. 'Think I look like Indiana Jones in this?'

She almost snorted. 'Let me tell you, if we get into this jungle and get chased by a giant ball or strange people shoot poison darts at us, you're in trouble.'

He shrugged. 'You forget. I know what your weakness is now. I can get out of just about anything with a piece of that chocolate cake.'

Hiro led them slowly on a well-worn path through the jungle. Caleb had been afraid that Tristan might be a little bored on the tour but

Hiro went out of his way to entertain their son. As they wound their way through the dark green trees he slid his hand into Addison's. She didn't object; in fact, she seemed to start chatting even more.

The jungle was full of things they would never have found on their own. Hiro pointed out ginger, ylang-ylang, vanilla, wild hibiscus, mango and coconut trees. 'Once we get back to the road, we'll find the stall with the real frozen coconuts and you can taste how delicious they really are.'

'Where does he get his energy from?' whispered Addison. 'He's like a supercharged battery.'

Caleb nodded. 'I know he whispered to Tristan earlier, but I kind of wish I could turn down the volume a little. I'm exhausted just listening to him.' He looked down to Addison. They'd been in the jungle for about twenty minutes now and the heat was slowly building around them. 'Hey, are you feeling okay?'

She slapped her hand gently against his chest. 'Quit fussing. I'm fine.'

He pretended to stagger. 'Hey, I just want to check that you'll be able to carry me out of here.'

She laughed. 'Not a chance. And anyway—' she glanced over her shoulder to see if anyone else was listening '—if I manage to shake you off in here I get to eat all the chocolate cake myself.'

He stopped dead and pressed his hand against his heart. 'Oh, no. That's brutal.'

She raised her eyebrows. 'You married a mercenary. Live with it.'

Tristan had walked on with Hiro and they'd stopped just ahead. 'Welcome,' shouted Hiro, 'to one of my favourite archaeological sites on the islands. The turtle petroglyphs.'

They all stepped forward. Giant boulders were sitting next to a little rock pool. The ancient carvings of turtles were faint but clearly visible. Some of the boulders were grey and some were clearly coral.

'How on earth did they get them up here?' asked Addison.

Hiro tapped his nose. 'No one actually knows. It's a mystery. They think they've been here for over a thousand years.' He threw up his hands. 'Imagine, a thousand years ago someone sitting in the jungle, carving this turtle with such care and attention to detail. A thousand years later it is still here. What do we have today that we think will survive a thousand years?'

'This place is amazing,' whispered Addison. 'I can almost picture someone doing it.'

Caleb smiled. She was enjoying this. He'd

been a little nervous that it wouldn't have lived up to expectations and they should actually just have spent the day on the beach, but Hiro was an entertaining guide and no part of the tour had been too taxing yet. He dropped a kiss on her head but then she surprised him. She tilted her chin up to him and kissed him on the mouth.

It was the briefest kiss—only a second. But it sent a jolt straight through him. A buzz. A connection. Something he'd been longing for since she'd looked him in eye and given him that ultimatum. Since he'd realised he was in danger of losing his wife, losing his family.

And the buzz had been initiated by her. It was almost a relief. She still felt something. There was something still there.

He'd been worried. Addison seemed to have put up invisible barriers. Ones that he had no idea how to penetrate or break down. Maybe they weren't quite so impenetrable as he feared.

He needed to talk to her. He needed to tell her why he'd been avoiding her. Why he'd been avoiding the conversation about more kids. Nothing would make him happier than to have another Tristan running around. He just didn't want to lose his wife in the process. If it was the choice between Addison or more kids, she would win every time.

Their walk back through the jungle to the

road was at a leisurely pace. Hiro piled them all back into the Jeep and drove just a little further down to one of the roadside stalls. There, they all sampled the half-coconuts, filled with frozen and iced coconut. It was delicious. But after a few sips through a straw Addison handed hers back over and made a face.

'You don't like it?'

Hiro pulled a flask from his back pocket. 'Would you like to add some rum?'

The other guests held out their coconuts straight away. 'What do you think?' Caleb smiled at Addison. 'Might make it more appealing.'

She shook her head. 'No, no, thanks. Not for me.'

He shrugged and finished his drink quickly. The rest of the tour moved along at a pleasant pace. Hiro showed them a huge variety of guns and cannons left from World War II. They were dotted all over the island. Then he drove them down a narrow winding road that ran along the edge of the island.

'Any idea where we're going?' Addison put her head on Caleb's shoulder.

Caleb shook his head. 'I'm guessing that this is the magical-mystery part of the tour.'

It didn't take long for a sign to come into

view. 'Here we are,' shouted Hiro. 'Welcome to my family pearl farm.'

He ushered them out of the Jeep and into the nearby shop sitting right on the edge of the lagoon. It was a perfect setting and as they watched some other tourists with snorkels and masks appeared at the wooden jetty in the water. All were clutching something in their hands.

'What are they doing, Daddy?' asked Tristan.

It didn't take long to realise. He knelt down next to his son. 'I think they've been diving in the lagoon for oysters.'

'What do you need an oyster for?' Tristan looked confused.

Addison gave a knowing smile. 'This place is called a pearl farm, honey. Some of those oysters will contain black pearls, like the ones on that sign—' she pointed next to her '—or like the ones in the cabinet over there.'

Even though it was afternoon and the sun was high in the sky, Hiro's energy hadn't diminished at all. 'Who would like to dive for their own pearl? I have equipment here that you can all use. Come on over, folks.'

Addison had moved across to the glass-fronted cabinets showing all the black-pearl jewellery. It was beautiful and there was a jeweller working in full view, mounting pearls in silver or gold to make a variety of items.

Tristan watched in wonder as one of the latest batch of divers came in and opened his oyster revealing a tiny black pearl.

'Can we get one, Daddy? Let's get one for Mummy.'

He bent down again. 'I'm not sure that every oyster has a pearl.'

Tristan glanced at Addison, then leaned forward and whispered, 'But let's try anyway.'

Caleb rolled his eyes. 'What do you think?' he asked Addison.

She gave a little shrug. 'Well, we're here now. I'm all for supporting local businesses.' Then she winked. 'Plus, I'm not the one that will get wet.'

Caleb grimaced as he changed into a pair of swim shorts that Hiro handed him, wondering who'd worn them before. Addison walked Tristan down the jetty and sat with her feet dangling in the water. She had a change of clothes for Tristan in her bag so just took off his socks, shoes and T-shirt and covered him in suncream. Caleb jumped into the lagoon, holding onto the jetty edge, and waited until the rest of the guests were ready too.

Hiro swam up alongside. 'I'll keep the little guy on the surface—' he handed her a kid's life jacket '—while your husband dives for the oyster.' He pulled a pair of goggles over Tristan's head. 'We'll watch your daddy go down to the bottom.'

Tristan clapped his hands with excitement. He was beginning to turn into a water baby. Not that Caleb minded. He'd never leave his four-year-old near water but both he and Addison had noticed how confident Tristan was getting. As long as one of his parents was near he would happily try and swim in the lagoon or the pool and he was doing really well. The swimming pool wasn't a place that Caleb had frequently taken his son back in London. But it was definitely something to reconsider. Addison was sitting directly above him as he bobbed in the water. 'How about we get a family membership to that new gym back home? It's got a swimming pool and I'm sure it does kids' swimming lessons.'

She tilted her head to the side and lifted her sunglasses to look at him. 'Swimming lessons would be good for him. It would be even better if we could go in the pool with him afterwards.'

'We'll both take him. Or I'll take him if you want a break.' It would be good to spend some time with Tristan alone. When he'd found out they were expecting a little boy he'd had all these great ideas about things he could do with his son. Because of work, most of them hadn't got off the ground.

Addison licked her lips and put her sunglasses back in place. 'That sounds good.'

He almost sighed with relief. She hadn't been accusatory. She hadn't mentioned all the times he'd let them down before. The tension between them definitely seemed to be lessening.

'Come on over, folks. Let's find us some pearls.'

Hiro came and put his arms around Tristan and guided the rest of the party a little way from the jetty. They treaded water for a few minutes as Hiro gave them some instructions as to where to dive to find the pearls. He made it sound relatively easy. 'These are the finest pearls in the world. The fragile black-lipped oyster, the *pinctada margaritifera*, produces our beautiful black pearls. Remember, that these pearls have taken two years to produce.' He was still holding onto Tristan. 'These pearls are one of the wonders of the world. When a tiny foreign substance gets inside an oyster it annoys it— like having an itch. Black lip oysters are very particular, they only react to one thing—a tiny round piece of oyster shell harvested from the Mississippi River. The oyster needs to scratch so it produces something called nacre. Over two years the layers of nacre build up—producing a pearl.'

He smiled widely at the people treading water

around him. 'Choose carefully—' he wagged his finger '—because not every oyster will contain a pearl. And our pearls can be five different colours. Who will get a black one?'

Tristan was bobbing away happily in his life jacket, his little legs kicking beneath him. 'You have to pick the right one, Daddy,' he said seriously.

'No pressure, then?' Caleb smiled. He turned in the water towards Hiro. 'You'll take care of him while I dive? He can go back to the jetty with Addison.'

Hiro shook his head. 'He's fine with me. Go and pick the right oyster. Tristan and I will watch you. Won't we?'

Tristan nodded happily and Caleb took a few seconds to take some deep breaths. The lagoon was a little deeper here—but the oysters weren't on the bed of the lagoon; instead there were four farming sections spread out around the lagoon, each anchored by rope to a bottom. Each section had around twenty-two lines attached, with four to six oysters attached to each line. They were all invited to dive down under the supervision of Hiro, unhook one line, and then bring it to the surface to find out what was inside.

Caleb gave Addison a wave before he dived. She was leaning back on the jetty letting the sun's rays warm her face. She gave him a smile and waved back. It warmed him, spreading heat through his body in the cool water. If he didn't have a black pearl in this oyster he would keep diving until he got one. He didn't care what the cost was. It didn't matter that Addison probably didn't care either way. He wanted to do it for her. It was a tiny little thing. But for them, it would be a little piece of history. She'd have something from Bora Bora, something that he'd got for her. It was unique. Just as she was.

The guy next to him dived, quickly followed by his wife. He sucked in a deep breath and dived down through the clear water. All their other diving excursions had been in relatively shallow water. It was surprising—the light from above was almost like a spotlight inside the lagoon. He could see clearly all the way down. By the time he reached the section with lines his lungs had already started to burn a little. He unclipped the nearest line. He knew the size of the oysters had no bearing on the size of the pearl inside and he pushed back up quickly, gasping as he broke the surface.

'Daddy! What did you get?'

He let the water stream off his face and took a few breaths. Hiro gave him a nod. It only took a few moments for the rest of the participants to surface. 'Everyone back over to the jetty and we'll go inside to open the oysters.'

Caleb kept pace with Hiro as he swam Tristan back to the jetty. Addison lifted their son out of the water, towelling him dry and changing his clothes.

Caleb raised his eyebrows, gave a shudder and tugged at his swim shorts. 'Give me two minutes until I get into my own clothes.' He ducked into the changing room at the shop and quickly pulled his T-shirt and shorts back on. He was still wet but didn't really care. When he came out Tristan and Addison were standing next to one of the counters talking to a female assistant.

'Look, Daddy, this is yours.'

Tristan pointed proudly at one of the oysters and Addison folded her arms and teased, 'If it's empty, you're in trouble.'

The female assistant gave him a nod. 'I'm Meherio. I'm going to show you how we harvest the oysters.' She picked up the one that Caleb had brought ashore and gave them all a smile. 'This little beauty is yours and we have to treat it with care.'

She took a few minutes gently clamping the oyster into a vice. Then, she pried the bivalve open just enough to gently fish around to find the gem. She turned to them and whispered, 'We do this carefully because a good oyster can keep creating pearls for up to seven years.

Our pearls actually come in five colours—blue, green, eggplant, peacock and gold. Only a few pearls are actually black. Most are a dark shade of green.'

Caleb realised he was holding his breath as she gently manoeuvred the pearl out from the oyster. He glanced towards Addison and Tristan, who were both holding their breaths and had their hands clasped in front of their chests. He couldn't resist; he pulled out his phone and snapped a picture.

'It's black!' shouted Tristan. 'It's black.'

'Not quite,' said Meherio as she held it between tweezers and inspected it in the light. 'But it's almost there.' She laid the pearl down on a piece of velvet in front of them.

It was odd. It was as if they were all mesmerised by the pearl he'd pulled from the lagoon. Meherio was obviously used to the effect the pearls had on people. She kept talking in a low voice. 'The lustre or reflective quality of the pearl's surface, along with its number of imperfections, are the key in determining its value.' She pulled out a ruler and measured the pearl. 'It's large.' Her smile was wide, revealing her perfect white teeth. 'Around fifteen millimetres.'

'Can I touch it?' Addison asked, her finger poised above it.

'Of course,' said Meherio. 'It's yours.' She glanced at Caleb. 'At least I expect it is.'

Caleb bent over to watch as she rolled the pearl gently on the velvet. It looked like an oil spill, with a rainbow of colours reflecting across its surface depending on the way she tilted it.

'Would you like to take it the way it is, or make it into a piece of jewellery? Our own jeweller can give you advice on what would work best for your pearl.'

'A necklace.'

They both said it at once.

Their gazes met, smiles on both of their faces. For a few seconds everything felt perfect between them. Everything felt the way it should. The way it was supposed to be.

This was the woman he loved with his whole heart. He could never imagine her not being in his life. He could never love anyone else the way he loved Addison.

It was simple.

They were meant to be.

He threaded his fingers through hers. 'Would your jeweller be able to mount the pearl for us?'

Meherio indicated the other side of the store. 'Come with me. You can choose silver or gold and our jeweller will mount the pearl for you while you watch.'

Caleb felt in his shorts pocket for his credit

card. He didn't really care what the cost of all this was going to be. For him the experience was already priceless.

Addison stood watching as the jeweller worked, leaning back against Caleb. His hand snaked around her middle. He liked this. He liked the fact that she felt comfortable enough to not think about what she was doing, but after a few seconds she closed her hand over his and moved his hand a little upwards.

He had a quick glance around the shop. He could hardly touch his wife's breast in public. So he just laughed and nuzzled in at her neck. 'Are you sure you didn't have any rum?'

She turned around towards him. 'Oh, I'm sure.' She paused for a second. 'Thank you.'

'What for?'

'For this. For today. It's felt…different.'

The jeweller gave him a nod and held up the pearl pendant on a long gold chain that Addison had chosen. 'Thank you,' said Caleb as he took it.

He moved behind her again and swept her hair away from the back of her neck. She looked up into the mirror in front of them, watching his actions with a hint of a smile. He opened the clasp on the chain and held the pendant in front of her, bringing it back slowly until it touched her skin. She didn't move. Didn't touch it. Just kept watching him in the mirror.

He lowered the pendant oh-so-slowly until it rested just above her cleavage, and fastened the clasp. Even from this position he could see the lustre and rainbow of reflections as her chest moved up and down with her breaths.

She was still watching him in the mirror. 'Thank you,' she said softly, in a voice that felt only for him. 'I love it.'

He bent to her ear and put his hands on her shoulders. 'You're worth it. You're worth a thousand of them.'

This was what was important.

This was the message he was trying to get through to his wife. He could see in the mirror that she was staring off into the distance now— as if her mind was lost on something else.

Was she really listening?

# CHAPTER NINE

'THIS WAY, MADAM. I'm sure we'll have something to suit you.'

As they opened the door to the room Addison was nearly blinded by sequins. Dozens of full-length dresses hung from hangers evenly spaced around the walls.

Addison held up her hands. 'Where did you get all these?'

Marisha, the resort employee, shrugged. 'Some people bring them on holiday, learn about the ball and decide to leave them behind. We had one holidaymaker who worked as a designer in New York. She sent us some dresses as a gift. Another woman worked in a designer boutique that was going to close. They shipped us all their remaining stock.'

Addison was smiling like a kid in a sweetie shop. 'This is fantastic. So, I just try a few, pick one and pay the hire fee?'

Marisha nodded. She pointed to a rack in the

corner. 'Those dresses are already reserved.' Then she held out her hands. 'Everything else is yours to choose from.' She walked over to a rail. 'We arrange by size. So, find your size, pick a dress you like and feel free to try it on.'

Addison nodded and moved over to the rails quickly finding her size. These dresses were every bit as beautiful as anything she had at home. She picked up a floor-length red dress. Red wasn't usually a colour that she wore. 'Can I try this one?'

Marisha swished open a set of deep purple velvet curtains. The opposite wall was covered in long mirrors. 'You can try in here. Do you need a hand?'

Addison shook her head just as the pager at Marisha's belt sounded. She glanced at it. 'If you're fine, I'll go and check what this is and be back in five minutes.'

Addison smiled. 'No problem. I'm sure I'll still be here.'

She closed the curtain behind her and slipped off her clothes. The dress was heavier than it looked on the hanger—probably because of the amount of sequins on it. And it had tiny little straps—she'd need to rethink her underwear.

She stepped into the dress and pulled it up. The zip was at the side. And that was the problem.

As soon as she started to pull the zip up she

realised she was in trouble. There was no way she wanted to force it and when she glanced in the mirror and realised how figure hugging it made the dress, her stomach was really obvious.

She needed to go up a size.

She slipped her own dress back over her head and padded out on bare feet to find something else. The red hadn't really suited. She needed something that suited her skin tone a little better.

There was plenty to choose from in the size up. She picked out a silver dress and decided to give it a go. The back was a little unusual—a low cowl back that caught the eye.

To her relief, this time the dress zipped easily. It was still figure hugging but because there was more room, it just made her look more curvy, enhancing her slightly larger breasts and widening hips without focusing on her stomach.

The thin straps and cowl back meant any bra would be out of the question, but the dress was supportive enough on its own.

'Oh, Mrs Connor, that's just beautiful.'

Addison jumped at the voice. Marisha had returned. She had her hand up at her face. 'Pick that one,' she urged.

She turned and looked back in the mirror. Once she'd got past the bling, the dress was actually really flattering. Marisha darted over to the corner and a pile of boxes. 'What shoe size are you? We'll have something that suits.'

Addison told her and a few seconds later Marisha pulled some high-heeled strappy silver sandals from a box. 'What about these?'

Addison smiled as she stepped over. They were just the perfect height to stop her full-length dress from dragging on the ground. 'Thank you. You better tell me what the charge will be for these items.'

Marisha gave her a nod and printed off a receipt. 'We actually ask that you pay over at the other resort. It all goes to their charity. You can pay for the hire at the same time you purchase your entry to the ball on the night.'

Addison glanced towards the other dresses on the reserved rail. 'So, do I just collect it on the night?'

'That's right. Someone will be here from six o'clock onwards. Just bring the receipt I printed for you, pick up the dress and have a great time.'

Addison touched the strap on her shoulder. 'I almost don't want to take it off.' She gave her head a shake. 'But I must. Give me five minutes.'

She ducked back behind the curtain and slid the dress off. Let them go to the ball. Let them dance as they used to and have fun as they used to.

Reality could wait another few days.

* * *

Caleb was pacing around and giving the occasional tug at the unfamiliar dress shirt. The suit was fine. It was made to measure—for someone that wasn't him. He wasn't sure he liked the whole 'hire a suit' business but since he couldn't go to a ball wearing a polo shirt, shorts and baseball boots he didn't really have any other options.

The sitter had arrived an hour ago. Tristan had been ecstatic. Should he be worried that his kid was so happy to see someone else? Kohia was a natural. She'd been playing with the wrestlers within a few minutes and Tristan couldn't be happier.

Addison was being a little secretive. She hadn't shown him what was in the dress bag she'd brought in the bungalow a little earlier and had disappeared into the bedroom to get ready.

Most of the other couples they'd met in the resort were going to the ball too. He glanced at his watch again. They'd all agreed to meet in the reception area—if Addison didn't hurry up they would be late.

A few seconds later the door to the bedroom swung open. Caleb caught his breath. She was stunning.

Her blonde hair hung in loose curls over her shoulders and the silver floor-length dress highlighted what a great figure his wife had. Every time she moved it glistened and shimmered and when she turned around to pick up her bag and he saw the back view he knew exactly where every set of eyes would be tonight.

She shot him a beaming smile and walked straight over to him. 'Who knew my husband could scrub up so well?' she teased as her perfume drifted around him.

Her green eyes were outlined with a little black and she had some pink lipstick on. He bent down and whispered in her ear. 'I've changed my mind about the ball. Let's just split to the over-water bungalow.'

She threw back her head and laughed, giving him a glimpse of her killer cleavage. It must be the dress—or some weird kind of bra—Addison's boobs didn't usually look so big. He felt like a teenager. He just wanted to touch them.

She crooked her arm towards him. 'Are we ready?'

'You're stunning.' The words just came straight out.

Her smile spread from ear to ear and he could see genuine happiness shining from her eyes.

Wow. When was the last time he'd stopped to notice just how gorgeous his wife was? And it wasn't that Addison didn't take care of herself at home—she did. But, by the time he left for work or got back in the evenings Addison was generally in bed. To make it worse, his mind was usually still full of work and the things he had to do—emails to send, a conference call to Japan at some time in the middle of the night, or share prices to check.

He sucked in a breath. *This* was what he should be paying attention to.

Maybe it was time to look at the business again? Harry had already dropped a few hints. They'd gone through three assistants in the last seven months. The amount and pressure of work seemed to wear people down in record time. At least his secretary was still there. She didn't seem to have any problem telling him exactly what her hours were and that she would stick to them.

He needed to pull that pile of CVs out of the drawer. A few had been personal recommendations from colleagues—people he trusted.

They could do with another partner and an assistant for each partner. They were lucky. Their office space was ample. They could do that. Making those kinds of changes wouldn't even have a detrimental effect on their income. They needed help more than they needed extra income.

They needed their lives back.

He'd sound out Harry when they got home—see if he agreed.

He slipped his arm into Addison's and they both said goodnight to Tristan. The sun had already started setting, sending orange and red streaks lighting up the sky behind the lagoon. By the time they reached the other resort it would be dark.

They walked quickly through the winding paths to the resort reception. Most of the other couples were waiting, with a few others joining a couple of minutes later. There must have been around a hundred people ready to go and join the ball. One of the resort staff met them all and, instead of taking them along the main path, he showed them another route that led to a gate between the two resorts that was usually hidden. It made the walk much shorter. 'Thank goodness,' breathed Addison. 'I wasn't quite sure how it would feel in these heels.'

Caleb nudged her. 'I could have always given you a piggyback.' Then his eyes ran up and down the length of her dress and he broke into a smile. 'But somehow I don't think in that dress it would quite work.'

Even though the evening was warm she gave a little shudder. It was almost as if she could read every single illicit thought he currently had in his mind. Their eyes fixed together for a few seconds. She raised her eyebrows. 'We're going to the ball,' she reminded him.

'Darn it.'

As they walked through to the next-door resort there was a collective gasp around them. The whole place was lit up like a Mardi Gras.

Music floated through the air towards them. First, the sounds of an outdoor Hawaiian band, greeting guests as they arrived with multi-coloured leis, then, as they neared the main complex, the sounds of an elegant concert band lured them inside.

Smartly dressed waiters were holding silver trays packed with drinks. Caleb automatically picked up two glasses of champagne and handed one to Addison. She was looking around in wonder.

In some ways it was like being back in London. The room was full of gentlemen in tuxedos and women in glittering floor-length dresses. They certainly knew how to throw a ball.

There were information stands in the hallways, telling the guests about breast cancer, along with posters of different people with their stories underneath. Caleb tightened his grasp on Addison's hand while his stomach threatened to land on his shoes. He was watching her carefully. Looking for any sign that would hint that she was affected by something similar.

But how on earth would he know? Addison's sister had died of ovarian cancer. Any one of these posters telling each person's story could bring a tear to her eye. That was why she was so good at all this.

Sure enough, she started to read all the stories. Twelve women and two men. Every single one was touching. Some had an early diagnosis and some had a late diagnosis. Some had ignored signs as they were too busy with life.

That struck a horrible chord. One of the men affected was just a few years older than him. He'd noticed a tiny lump as he showered but as he was a regular at the gym had put it down to a muscle strain or injury. He couldn't afford to take time off work as he was so busy. It had taken him months to attend his doctor.

Most of the stories were of survivors, a few, sadly, were not. As they walked along the row he slid his arm around Addison's waist and pulled her closer to him.

She didn't appear to be sad. In fact, she engaged with every one of the people manning the stands and spoke passionately about raising awareness of the different types of cancer. The ball was raising funds for a mammogram for island residents. Although the local hospital was well-equipped and could deal with emergencies, it didn't have a mammogram for screening. Residents had to attend Tahiti if they wished to have breast screening and the ball was to aid funds to start the screening service on the island.

Caleb took a few minutes to pay for their tickets, clothing hire and leave a generous donation. They were lucky. They were in a position to be able to do that—as were most of the people attending the ball tonight.

Addison was still chatting. She was swapping emails with someone and agreeing to send them some materials from her charity. She'd hardly touched her champagne, her fingers just stroking up then down the chilled glass.

He put his empty glass on a waiter's tray and picked up another as he waited for her. She joined him a few minutes later, bright-eyed and breathless. 'Sorry, I couldn't stop talking. Everything they are doing here is wonderful.'

Animated. That was how she was right now because she was involved in an area she was passionate about.

'Do you want something different to drink? A cocktail?'

She glanced down at her glass and shook her head. 'This is fine.'

They moved inside the main ballroom. The band were sitting on the stage all dressed in black and white, with the conductor in front of them. The sound reverberated around the room.

It was loud but elegant. They were playing Hollywood show tunes and some people were already singing along.

White linen tablecloths covered the round tables around the dance floor, decorated with a bright array of tropical flowers. On either side of the ballroom, doors opened out into the resort gardens to allow the air to circulate freely.

A huge buffet was spread out on long tables. This wasn't a formal sit-down dinner. People were free to choose what and when they wanted to eat. Several of the couples from their own resort were already eating and gave them a wave.

'Want to sit down?' Caleb asked.

She put her hand on his arm. 'Not really. Not yet.' She glanced towards the dance floor. A few couples were dancing already.

Caleb shook his head. 'Oh, no. You want to dance already? We just got here.'

Dancing wasn't his forte—never had been. It had been one of the things that his friend Reuben always teased him about. He usually only danced when Addison pulled him up on the dance floor. The rest of the time he was happy just to spectate.

Addison turned towards him. As she did the coloured strobe lights in the room caught her dress, turning her into a shimmering rainbow of colour. She looked down and laughed. She held out her hands. 'Ever get the impression that someone is trying to tell you something?'

He must have hesitated too long because she looked around the room, tossing her hair over one shoulder and then the other. 'I'm sure I can find someone in here who will dance with me.'

That was all he needed. He set down his champagne glass and grabbed her hand, pulling her towards the dance floor and praying that nothing remotely fast would come on.

He was lucky. Cole Porter's 'I've Got You Under My Skin' started playing. This, he could manage. This meant that he got to hold the woman he loved and just sway.

Addison was in his arms instantly, his hands on her hips and her hands on his shoulders. She sang along as they swayed. An older man and woman near them started gliding around the dance floor as if they were on ice.

He leaned forward and mumbled in Addison's ear. 'There's always one.'

'Maybe I should send you to dance lessons?'

'How about if I promise to do it for our tenth anniversary?'

He moved a little faster and spun her around, catching her off balance and using the opportunity to pull her even closer to him.

Her eyes widened. She looked surprised and gave a little bite to her bottom lip.

What did that mean? It was like an icy wind rippling over his skin. Did Addison not intend to be around for their ten-year anniversary? Or was it something out of her control? His brain was playing tricks on him again. Pulling ridiculous thoughts out of places that usually didn't exist. He was normally so rational. But it seemed that somewhere along the line a tiny element of fear had embedded itself within him.

Fear of losing Addison.

It was unthinkable and chilled him to the bone.

He plastered a smile on his face. It was a simple bite of the lip. It meant nothing. His wild imagination needed to be put back into its box. He'd done exactly what Addison had asked—he'd come on this holiday. He was spending as much time with them both as possible. And he was enjoying it.

Once he got home he'd speak to Harry. He'd try and reduce his hours at work. He'd make sure he spent more time with Addison and with Tristan. Maybe they could even think about adding to the family? If they were both thinking of reducing their hours it could be a possibility.

Addison was still staring at him. 'You'll learn to dance for our anniversary?'

He spun her around again. 'Of course I will. Wait and see. I'll be the next Johnny and you can be the next Baby.' He laughed and spun her around again. 'I won't leave you sitting in a corner.'

She put her hand up to her forehead. 'The thought of you in tight black trousers trying to jive is making me feel faint.'

She smiled as the music came to a close. 'Feed me, Caleb. Give me time to recover.'

He slid his arm back around her waist and walked over to the buffet. There was a huge variety of food. Chefs were waiting behind the serving area, with fish sizzling in the pans in front of them, restocking the buffet constantly. Off to the side was a large table of desserts. Addison picked up a plate and started working her way along. She wasn't a huge eater, only putting some spiced chicken and a little fish on her plate. Caleb had filled his plate completely by the time he reached the end of the buffet table and could happily have gone back for more.

They wandered over to one of the large tables and sat down. The band was still playing and the ballroom seemed to be getting busier by the second. A waiter appeared beside them. 'Would you like some champagne, or something else?'

Caleb wasn't a huge champagne drinker. 'Can we change to something else?'

Addison gave a nod just as another waiter passed carrying a tray with blue cocktails.

'They look interesting. We'll have two of those, thanks,' he said quickly.

Addison proceeded to choke on her mouthful of food. 'Hey.' He patted her back. 'What's up?'

She frowned and grabbed the waiter just before he left. 'Can I have some water too, please?' She turned back to Caleb. 'I'm not sure about the blue things. I've a sneaky suspicion it might be gin—and you know I hate that.'

He shook his head. 'No. I bet they're rum. All the cocktails around here are rum—and you love those.'

He gave a little nod to another couple who came and sat down beside them. Their plates were overloaded.

The guy reached over with his hand and spoke in a strong American accent. 'Hi, I'm Steven Shankland, this is my wife, Mindy.' He quirked his head. 'Haven't seen you two around here. Are you just visiting for the ball?'

Caleb stood up to shake the guy's hand. 'Yes, I'm Caleb Connor and this is my wife, Addison. You'll guess from the accent we're from the UK. We're staying at the resort next door with our son.'

Mindy looked up from her monster plate as Caleb hid a smile. She was stick thin. Was she really going to eat all that? 'What's the resort like? We considered it, but finally decided on this one.'

Addison smiled. 'It's exactly what I wanted—very peaceful. Our son is having a great time. We have a beach bungalow and an over-water bungalow with a glass panel in the floor. He's loving every second.'

Steven looked at her curiously. 'What do you guys do in the UK?'

Again, Caleb tried not to smile. He admired the directness of Americans. But he wasn't going to give too much away. Addison shot him a slightly anxious glance. He could tell she didn't want this to turn into a business conversation.

'I have my own business in London, dealing mainly in finance. Addison runs a charity for ovarian cancer. What about you—what part of America are you from?'

Although Steven was curious, Caleb had met lots of men like him before. They always preferred it when a conversation came back around to them.

The waiter appeared with the two blue cocktails and a glass of water for Addison, taking Steven's order before he left.

Steven had launched into a great story, all about living in Boston and being a surgeon.

Mindy barely lifted her head as she continued to plough through the plateful of food.

Caleb slid his hand underneath the table to give Addison's leg a squeeze. Her hand disappeared under the table too and she interlocked her fingers with his. For some reason he didn't want to share his wife tonight. In the past, they'd both been pretty sociable and been happy to be in anyone's company.

But time now felt special. Selfish or not, he only wanted to spend it with Addison.

The waiter came back with Steven and Mindy's drinks and Caleb pulled Addison up, grabbing their plates. 'Excuse us a second, we're off to restock.'

'Thank goodness,' breathed Addison as they wove their way through the crowd.

Caleb dumped the plates and pulled her towards the dessert table. It was piled high with puddings, cakes, tarts, profiteroles, ice cream and fresh fruit.

'What would you like?' He selected a fork and speared a tiny piece of chocolate cake, holding it out towards her. She smiled and leaned forward, eating it quickly.

'Delicious,' she declared. 'But that's actually enough.' She moved a little closer. 'What I'd actually like to do is dance with my husband again.'

The noise level around them had increased and the band seemed to have got louder too. The dance floor was busier. More and more people were up there—some of them looked professional.

Caleb took a deep breath. 'Okay, then, if that's what you want to do…'

Addison nodded her head. 'Absolutely. That's what I want to do.'

Nothing could compare to the way she felt in her husband's arms and she was the complete focus of his attention. She knew Caleb didn't like to dance but he could manage a slow shuffle around the floor and that was good enough for her.

It was so easy to slip her arms around his neck, press her body up against his and let his lips come into contact with hers. His hands traced little circles on her bare back, sending a million little pulses in every direction. The music, the surroundings, the people around them all blurred out of focus. The only person she was paying attention to was her husband.

It finally felt as if she had got him back. It finally felt as if this was the man she'd fallen in love with. And everything should be perfect now.

Except it wasn't.

Twice tonight she'd made an excuse about alcohol. She hadn't touched her first glass of champagne, putting it down on another table the first time that they'd danced. The blue cocktail was still sitting at their old table untouched.

She hated that. She hated that she hadn't been honest with her husband. But she hadn't been ready to. And now she was.

His lips met hers again and she closed her eyes. This was what she had missed. This was what she remembered. Every inch of Caleb's body, the breadth of his shoulders, the way he held her in his arms and the feel of his lips against hers.

She moved her hands from around his neck and slid them under his jacket and along the thin material of his shirt. One hand moved from her back, catching the back of her head and tangling in her hair. The other was still tracing little circles on her back. It was hypnotic; it was mesmerising. If she could capture this moment and just keep it here, she would.

The song finished and she took a step back, conscious that people could be watching them. She hated that she might spoil things—spoil what they'd just recaptured. But real life was knocking persistently at the door. She needed her husband's support right now—she needed to tell him what they might be facing.

Caleb's brown eyes were fixed directly on hers. 'Wanna get out of here?' he mumbled.

'Sure.' It sounded so definite, but her heart was racing. Her guilt complex wasn't going to let her keep this secret any longer. Now she had back the man she wanted she had no excuse.

His hand closed over hers and he walked with big strides towards the open doors to the gardens. She almost had to run to keep up.

The cooler night air hit them as soon as they walked outside. Caleb shrugged off his jacket and put it around her shoulders. The gardens at this resort were just as beautiful as those next door.

The smell was intensely fragrant, enticing her to lose herself further in the gardens. They were surrounded by delicate flowers like the white Tahitian *tiare*, along with colourful splashes of gardenia, jasmine, flowering vines of many species, and vibrant hibiscus in stunning shades.

'Listen to the birds,' she said as she looked around in wonder. It was almost like being at a private party.

'Look.' Caleb pointed as the birds darted first one way amongst the greenery, and then the other. Blue lorikeets, fruit doves, kingfishers and cuckoos were all around them.

'It's like being stuck in paradise,' she murmured.

'So it is,' he echoed, but when she turned back Caleb's eyes were on her and not the birds.

She held her breath. She had to tell him.

Then he laughed, put his hands on her hips and pulled her closer to him. He started to sway and sing at the same time. Caleb *never* sang.

They weren't in public now. No one could see them in amongst the green of the gardens. He kept his voice low, singing quietly, only to her. It seemed that Caleb had his own version of 'I've Got You Under My Skin'. His dancing was a bit freer too. He spun her around as he sang, lifting her up and letting her see the twinkle in his eyes. 'Caleb,' she squealed. 'What are you doing?'

It squeezed at her heart. It was like a whole new side of Caleb. One that had been revealed on a holiday where he'd finally managed to shake off the pressures of work. One that had given him the chance and space to be with his family again.

He was holding her under the arms, facing him, but up above the ground, up above his head. She was looking down and laughing because he was still singing to her. Their bodies were close together as he lowered her oh-so-slowly to the ground and she could feel every part of him.

Just when she thought he was finished, he

spun her around again then put her in a backward dip. Their faces were only inches from each other. She lifted her hands to his shoulders again. He was breathing heavily. She was guessing she wasn't as light as he remembered. His aftershave drifted towards her on a little gust of wind. It was the honeymoon one again. And it was definitely stirring up memories.

She reached up and touched his jaw, feeling the tiniest hint of stubble underneath her fingertips. He dropped a kiss on her lips and spun her upwards again at lightning speed until she was facing him.

Her head gave a momentary judder. She was feeling a tiny bit dizzy.

He noticed and smiled. 'Too much alcohol?'

Her heart stilled. She knew he was joking but she couldn't let the night end without being honest with him.

She took a deep breath and went ahead before she changed her mind again. 'Caleb, we need to talk. There's something I need to tell you.'

The evening had almost been perfect. Almost. Right up until that point he'd thought he was waltzing his gorgeous wife home and into bed again.

Then he'd seen her take a deep breath and fix her clear green eyes on his.

If this were a science-fiction movie time would have stopped at this point.

But it wasn't. It was here and now.

For so many days he'd wanted to know what was wrong with Addison. But for the first time in his life he felt afraid to actually hear the words.

There were too many possibilities. Too many outcomes that he might not like. She was sick. She didn't love him any more. She wanted to leave. She'd met someone else. All of them had crept into his head at some point and he'd pushed all of them away.

He kept his voice as steady as possible. 'What is it, Addison?'

But her voice wasn't steady. Her voice was shaking. 'I'm pregnant.'

What? *What?* 'What?' It was probably the last thing he'd expected to hear. Relief swept through him in an instant. She wasn't dying. She wasn't leaving. She did still love him. 'You're pregnant?' There was the briefest second of hesitation as all the fears he'd had about her being unwell again tried to clamour to the surface. But he pushed them away. Relief was still flooding through him. His wife wasn't ill. Anything else they could deal with. 'That's wonderful!'

He picked her up again and swung her around. Another Tristan. Or maybe even a little girl. It didn't matter. He would take either. Just as long as his family was in one piece.

He sat her down and touched her stomach, dropping to his knees and kissing it. 'Hello, baby, how are you?' He couldn't stop grinning. It was important that he didn't say anything to upset her. At some point, he'd sit down with her and talk—talk about why he had worries. They could plan ahead. But just not now. 'When are we due? How far along are you?'

His hand was still resting on her stomach. There was a definite slight bump. Why hadn't he noticed? Didn't women show a bit quicker with their second babies?

'Fifteen weeks tomorrow.' His head shot up; there was a definite waver in her voice. He stood up and caught her head in his hand.

'Hey? What's wrong? Fifteen weeks, that's nearly four months. Didn't you know—did you only just realise?'

It made sense to him. That could be the only possible reason she could be upset. His brain did the rapid calculations. 'So baby is due in November?'

He gave her a giant hug. 'That's brilliant, another Connor for Christmas.'

It was almost as if his brain had gone into overdrive. This was why she was pressing him not to work so hard. This was why she was

going to employ someone else at the charity.
Pieces of the puzzle were starting to fall into
place.

He put both his hands up to her cheeks. 'Don't
worry. Everything will be fine. I promise. I'll
speak to Harry when I get home. We'll see about
hiring another partner and some more associates. It's about time we expanded. I'll make sure
everything is in place before this baby arrives.'

He was so buzzed he could hardly think
straight, so when tears pooled in Addison's eyes
and one slid down her cheek he was astonished.

'I did know,' she whispered.

It was the expression on her face, the pain
in her eyes. None of this fitted with what she'd
just told him.

'What?' He pulled back. 'Then why didn't
you tell me?'

Addison's breathing was stilted. She couldn't
look him in the eye.

He put his hands on her shoulders. 'Why
didn't you tell me? Why didn't you tell me about
the baby?'

She brushed him off and took a few steps
away.

'Didn't you think I would be happy?'

She spun back around. 'That's just it, Caleb.
I didn't know. I don't know you any more. We
hardly see each other. Up until now, I don't re-

member when we last spent any time together.'
She shook her head. 'You'd already told me you
didn't want to have more kids.' She pressed her
hand on her stomach. 'Then, this happened. I
didn't know what to do.'

'What's that supposed to mean?' His raised
voice sent a bird shooting from a nearby bush
into the sky above. Adrenaline was surging
through him. 'Don't you want to have our baby?'

Her face crumpled. 'Of course I do. That's
not what I said.'

'So, what do you mean—*I didn't know what
to do*?'

The tears were flooding down her face now.
He hated to see Addison cry—always had—
but he couldn't stop the rage that was racing
through him.

She'd kept this from him. Something that
should be happy news they could share with
the world—she'd deliberately not told him.

Words couldn't even begin to describe how
much that hurt. Were they really so far apart
that his wife couldn't tell him she was pregnant?

Addison lifted her hand and wiped her eyes,
smearing mascara across her face. She straightened her back and looked at him. 'I didn't know
if I wanted to stay. I didn't how you'd feel about
another child when you'd said no before. I didn't
know if it was good to bring another child into

a marriage that is already so strained we can barely talk to each other. I want to be able to talk to my husband the way we used to. Not like we are now.'

He could tell she was trying her best to be strong but her voice was still shaking.

'You want to leave?' This night just got better and better.

She closed her eyes for a second. 'I thought I did. I thought you didn't have time for us any more.'

He ran his hands through his hair and took a few steps, trying to stifle his frustration. 'So, my crime is that I'm busy. I work too hard. I support my family. That's why you wanted to leave?'

He was struggling. He was really struggling with this. Part of him felt relief that she hadn't told him she'd met someone else. But the reality that she'd actually considered leaving him was devastating.

The thought of not seeing Addison and Tristan every day made part of him want to curl up and die.

Addison was shaking her head. 'You know how things have been, Caleb. Don't pretend that you don't.' She pointed down with her hand. 'This is the first time in about two years that you've actually been with us.' She pressed her hand over her heart. 'Been with me. Do you know how lonely I've been?'

'Do you know how lonely I've been? Do you know what it feels like to make another excuse to stay at work rather than come home, because you never know the reception you'll get?

'And have I passed the test? Have you changed your mind now you're actually telling me about our baby?'

She hesitated. She actually hesitated. She cleared her throat. 'We've talked about this. You said that you would stop working so hard. That you would make adjustments. I want us to be a family. I want us to be together. I love you, Caleb, but I'm not afraid to do this on my own. You've been taking us for granted. I need you to *want* me to be there. You've just told me you don't want to come home.'

'Of course I want you to be there. But I don't think this is about me wanting you. I think this is about you wanting me. Do you actually want me to be in your life?'

It was a horrible question to ask. A horrible thing to say out loud. His heart felt like putty in her hand.

Addison looked pale, or maybe it was the moonlight and the silver dress. She reached down and pulled her shoes from her feet. 'I can't do this. I can't do this any more. I'm too tired. I'm going back to the bungalow to sleep.'

He stepped forward. 'You can't go away now. You've kept one of the most important things in our life from me. It was as good as lying to me.'

This time Addison raised her voice. 'Do you know what? I tried to tell you. I tried, Caleb. I phoned you at work. I asked you if you'd be home for dinner that night. I dressed up—I put on the pink dress that you'd bought me and cooked you your favourite dinner. Then, I did what I did the first time. I put the pregnancy test under a silver dome, sat it at your plate setting and waited for you to come home.' She shook her head. 'Do you know what that feels like? To be so happy, so excited and dying to share the news?' She put her hands on her hips. 'Well, I waited, Caleb. I waited and I waited. I sat there for three hours waiting for you to come home. No phone call. No message. Nothing. And it made me realise just how you prioritised your life. Because even when your wife phones you, even when she asks you specially when you'll be home, as soon as you put down that phone it just vanishes from your mind.' She clicked her fingers. 'Poof! Just like that. How do you think that feels? So don't dare tell me that I lied to you by omission because you weren't there, Caleb, you just weren't there!'

He'd never heard Addison shout like this before. He'd never seen her so worked up. She was furious—and she wasn't finished yet.

'So don't you dare tell me I can't go away. I can. And I will.'

Her dress swished as she turned and disappeared along the path.

He should go after her. He knew he should.

But he just couldn't. They needed time apart. They needed space.

He heard muffled voices a little bit away. No doubt other guests had heard the shouting in the garden.

He tugged at the neck of the tuxedo shirt. It was driving him crazy.

He couldn't pretend he wasn't hurt. He couldn't pretend he wasn't angry. Those first few seconds of finding out Addison was pregnant again had been truly magical. But those few seconds had been snatched away with the realisation of everything else.

Something crept over him, like an icy cold hand sliding down his spine.

She hadn't answered. She hadn't answered that final question.

*Do you actually want me to be in your life?*

Had he left things too late to actually resolve? The champagne from earlier roiled in his stomach. He loved his wife. He loved his son. And he loved this baby too.

But was it all too late?

'Sir, are you all right?' It was one of the resort staff. Someone must have told them about the shouting.

'I'm fine,' he replied as he tugged off the bow tie and turned in the other direction.

The beach. That was where he'd go. It would be quiet. It would be empty. It would give him some time to think things through.

Because the last thing he was right now was fine.

# CHAPTER TEN

THE DRESS MADE it difficult to walk as quickly as she could. Parts of the path had tiny stones that jagged the soles of her feet but she didn't want to stop to put her shoes back on.

Things couldn't have gone worse. She'd turned a perfect evening into a nightmare. All because she'd felt overloaded with guilt.

She'd hurt him. She'd cut him to the bone and she realised that.

His reaction when she'd told him she was pregnant had made her realise what she'd done. He'd been happy. On a normal day it was the perfect reaction.

Sure, there had been a tiny second of hesitation. But he wasn't angry about the baby.

But when he'd asked when the baby was due her tongue had stuck to the top of her mouth. She'd had to admit the truth.

It would have been easy to say she'd just found out. It would have been easy and simpler to make up some feeble excuse as to why she hadn't noticed her periods had stopped.

But it wouldn't have been true. It wouldn't have brought everything to a head.

Maybe she should have lied. Maybe she should have said she'd just found out. But that would create more problems for her later.

Because no matter how hurtful it was, she had to let Caleb know that she'd thought about leaving.

It made her insides curl up. She knew exactly the effort he'd been making and she'd fallen a little bit more in love with him again every day.

She felt so guilty. Her husband had told her he didn't want to come home. He didn't want to come home to *her*. It hurt. It hurt because she knew why. She was distant with Caleb. She was cold. Their conversations were about Tristan's schedule. She'd been so fed up with him working that she never even asked him what kind of day he'd had any more. Just as he didn't ask her. She wanted things to change between them so badly. Being on Bora Bora made her feel as if they'd captured part of themselves again. The part that had been missing for the last year. They'd finally started to talk and communicate again. So, was she just about to ruin everything? Lying by omission. That was what he'd accused her of.

But she hadn't even told him the most important thing yet.

The fact that their baby was at high risk.

How would he react then?

She pressed her hands on her stomach.

He'd misunderstood her. When she'd said she didn't know what to do, he'd thought she was talking about the baby, not about them. And that horrified her.

Every bit as much as it had horrified him.

Trouble was it had made her angry and she'd started to vent all the pent-up frustrations of the last few years. She'd said things without thinking.

But she hadn't said the most important thing.

The bungalow was in sight. She took a deep breath and gave her face a wipe. She didn't want to go inside when it was obvious she had been crying.

She hadn't been lying. She was exhausted and she needed to lie down. Tiny thoughts in her brain were pushing their way forward again. The ones that made her take part of the blame for this situation. She didn't even want to acknowledge them. To think about them at all. The sooner she got to bed, the better.

Kohia was sitting on the sofa watching the TV as she came in. 'Hi, Mrs Connor. Tristan was a dream. He went to bed a couple of hours ago.'

'Thank you so much, Kohia. I really appreciate it.'

Kohia picked up her bag and walked to the door. 'No problem. I'll see Tristan at kids' club tomorrow.' She gave a little smile, 'By the way, you might find some wrestlers in his bed.'

Addison forced a smile. 'No problem. See you tomorrow.'

She let out a sigh as Kohia left and she closed the door behind her.

She unzipped the dress then put it back on the hanger. It was beautiful and for a short time she'd felt wonderful in it. But for now, it only reminded her of one of the worst nights of her life.

She didn't even wash her face. Just pulled on her nightie and climbed into bed with Tristan. She snuggled her arms around the little warm body.

Comfort. That was what she needed right now.

But it didn't stop the tears from falling again.

Caleb watched the sun rise on the beach again. He'd eventually moved along the beach, nearer the bungalow. But he just couldn't bring himself to go in.

He still felt too raw and the last thing he needed to do right now was cause another fight.

Watching the sun rise on this beach was getting to be a dangerous habit.

A little after seven the waiter appeared with the breakfast tray. His stomach growled but he didn't think he could eat right now.

The door to the bungalow opened and Addison appeared.

She had one of his T-shirts and a pair of shorts on. Her hair was tied on top of her head and she looked deathly pale. It was obvious she'd had as restless a night as he had.

She walked over towards him and sat down on the beach next to him.

She held out her hand. 'Don't say anything. Let me speak. I need to get this out there.'

What now? She'd cancelled his flight home?

She wasn't looking at him. She was staring out across the lagoon, watching the egrets trying to swoop down and catch fish.

'I didn't tell you everything last night. I didn't tell you the most important thing.'

There was more? He was struggling with the not-talking part. He wanted to say so much right now. But, last night's lesson was to try and listen instead of just reacting. It was already proving hard to learn.

'I got a call just before we left the house.'

He nodded. He remembered. He'd been on a call himself and hadn't paid too much attention.

She started tracing circles in the sand with her finger. 'It was my doctor—my obstetrician. He needed to talk to me about some tests.'

'What tests?' He couldn't help himself. There was no way he could keep quiet. His brain was starting to race again. There was something ominous about this.

'I'd had my baby scan. They do the nuchal screening test. The one where they measure the fluid at the back of the baby's neck. They take blood and use that, along with my age, to see if our baby is at high risk.'

He could remember parts of this. When she was pregnant with Tristan he'd held her hand through the scan. He could remember the sonographer fiddling to get the tiny measurement she'd needed for the scan. 'That's the test for Down's syndrome, isn't it?'

All the fine hairs on his arms stood on end. He turned to face her. His heart had started racing in his chest. 'Isn't it?'

She nodded. She opened her mouth to speak again and then stopped. Her hand was shaking as it traced the circles in the sand. He closed his hand over hers and tried to speak. 'What did the doctor tell you? Is our baby affected?'

She pulled her hand away, drawing her knees up to her chest and putting her hands over her face. 'I don't know. He told me our baby is at high risk.'

Panic seared through him. 'What does that mean? What's high risk?' He was trying to stay calm but it wasn't easy. He wanted to ask a hundred questions at once. He'd already been worried about how his wife would cope after delivering another baby. He hadn't even considered there could be extra complications. What if they were all just too much for Addison?

She turned to face him. This time she actually did look at him and it nearly broke his heart. The pain etched on her face was clear. She'd known this since just before they'd left. She'd had no chance to talk to anyone, to sit down and find out more. It seemed crazy. How had she managed to stay calm?

'For someone my age, normal risk would be around one in a thousand. Dr Mackay said my risk is one in one hundred and forty.'

Numbers. Caleb dealt with numbers at work every day. He was good with numbers. Numbers were what he based every business decision on.

But suddenly numbers didn't seem so secure.

The leap from one in a thousand to one in one hundred and forty seemed huge.

He felt stunned. It was as if someone had just taken the legs from under him—thank goodness he was sitting down.

Caleb gently stroked her cheek. 'What happens now?'

She pressed her lips together. 'Nothing. This is our baby. I love it already. I'm prepared to deal with whatever happens.'

He frowned. 'Addison? What did you think I meant? Are there other tests? Other things they need to do? Can we find out for sure?'

She shook her head. 'Dr Mackay asked me if I wanted an amniocentesis test. That would tell us for sure. But it carries a risk of miscarriage. I can't do it. I just can't.'

'Is there anything else they can do?'

She nodded. 'They can do a detailed scan at twenty weeks. It can look at the baby's facial features and all the vital organs. Some kids with Down's syndrome have cardiac problems—some babies require surgery straight away.'

'Oh, no.' He couldn't help it. The thought of their brand-new baby needing heart surgery straight away was terrifying.

He was silent for a moment, trying to process all the thoughts in his head. 'Addison, I don't know enough about this. I don't know enough about Down's syndrome. If this is what the future holds, then we need to find out more. We need to prepare ourselves and prepare Tristan.'

They were side by side on the beach but he'd honestly never felt so alone. He wrapped his arm around her shoulders and pulled her closer to him. After a few seconds she put her head on his shoulder and started to sob.

Nothing else mattered. Nothing else mattered but this.

It was overwhelming. It was staggering. He was racking his brains—trying to remember anything he could. There had been a boy at his junior school—Alec someone—his brother had Down's syndrome. But he was embarrassed to admit that all he could remember was that the little guy had worn hearing aids and had had a really happy disposition. That was it. Alec had been fiercely protective of his little brother—and also fiercely proud. Why hadn't he paid more attention—why didn't he know more?

He rubbed his hand up and down Addison's arm. 'You should have told me,' he said softly. 'You shouldn't have kept this to yourself.'

Her head shot up and there was a momentary flash of anger. 'How could I? You were just about to tell me that you weren't coming on holiday with us.'

She was right. Of course she was right. That was exactly what he'd been about to do. Until she'd given him the ultimatum.

And now he understood why. She'd already been stressed about the pregnancy. She'd already been worried about their marriage. The news about being high risk must have tipped her off the cliff edge she'd been dangling from.

She hadn't even been able to talk to him about it. Because she hadn't decided if she wanted to stay.

He took a deep breath and tried to think rationally.

'Let's take a minute. Let's talk about this. One in one hundred and forty sounds scary initially, but that also means that one hundred and thirty-nine times out of one hundred and forty our baby won't be affected. Those odds are pretty good.'

She raised her head. 'I know that. But it doesn't really make me any less scared.'

He squeezed her. 'I'm scared too. I'm terrified. I hate not knowing things. And I don't know enough about all this. I want to run screaming somewhere and find a computer so I can scan the Internet.'

She gave a little laugh. 'For once in your life you don't want Internet for work.'

He shook his head. 'No. I don't. I want to know how to plan ahead. I want to know what else we should do.' He paused for a second. 'Are you sure you don't want to have the amniocentesis?'

She shook her head fiercely but he lifted his hand. 'Hear me out. There's still another twenty-five weeks to go in this pregnancy. That's a long time to worry. A long time to not know what's ahead. I understand about the risks of miscarriage. Do you remember what they are?'

She shook her head again.

The sun-kissed look she'd had on her face a few days ago seemed to have vanished. It had been replaced by a pale and strained look, tiny wrinkles around her eyes and deep creases in her forehead. She was now wringing her hands in her lap. All he could see was stress. It simply oozed from every pore.

He sat back a little, trying to appear more relaxed. 'Okay. I don't know the risks so it's difficult to know if it's something we should consider.' He gave her a weak smile. 'Before I say this, I want you to know that you're gorgeous as always.'

She gave a sigh. 'Sure I am.'

'You're stressed. I'm not surprised. But I need to know if it's been the stress of keeping this secret that's made it worse, or if it's just the worry in general. I'm thinking about the next twenty-five weeks. I'm thinking of keeping our baby safe. If you're going to spend the next few weeks not sleeping and with your blood pressure through the roof then maybe we should think about the test. Is the not knowing actually going to make things worse?'

It felt like a reasonable question. It felt like the kind of discussions they should be having. Her voice wasn't quite so shaky this time. 'I think I've just been angry,' she said quietly. Her green eyes met his. 'Angry at everything. Angry at me. Angry at you. Angry at my blood test.'

She put her head in her hands again. 'And I've felt panicky.'

'Why?' He needed to coax her. He needed to get everything out there.

She bit her lip. 'It's not easy to say out loud, but we both know I struggled when Tristan was a baby. You were better at the night-time stuff than I was. You had more patience. I reached a point where I had to walk into another room because I couldn't stop him crying.' She stared off into the distance. 'And the rest.' Her fingers toyed with a little bit of hair at the side of her head. 'I felt numb then. It took me time to connect with Tristan. I felt useless. I felt as if I was failing as a mother and...' she met his gaze '...as a wife.'

He reached out and touched her. 'Addison, I've been scared too. When you mentioned having another baby I panicked. And I never panic.' He sucked in a deep breath. 'Last time around I felt as if you were slipping through my fingers and I couldn't do a damn thing to stop it. I might have worked regular hours then, but I was still at work all day. I could see you disconnecting. I could see you struggling. You were home all day with Tristan and I spent all day worrying about how I could try and help you get back to normal.' He shook his head. 'I phoned that health visitor so many times I'm sure she could have got me done for stalking.'

Her eyes were filling with tears again. 'That's why you didn't want to have more kids? Because of me?'

He nodded. 'Of course I want more kids. But what I also want is my wife. It was me who got you pregnant. It was me who did this to you. I was terrified you might feel like that again.'

'I'm sorry, Caleb. I'm sorry I didn't sit down and tell you straight away that I was pregnant. I'm sorry that the second I got that phone call from Dr Mackay I didn't call you over to listen too.'

He tilted up her chin towards him. 'Addison Connor, you are a great mum. Don't ever doubt that—not for a second. Tristan is lucky to have you and this baby will be too. I am going to be with you every step of the way. We're in this together. For ever.'

She wrapped her arms around herself and looked back to the horizon for a second. 'I was worried. Worried you wouldn't be around—not like the last time. And if I struggled with Tristan and he didn't have any health conditions...what if I'm not good enough now?'

'Addison, don't. Don't think like that. You are good enough. You're perfect. And you won't be on your own. I'll be there. I promise I'll be there. And Lara will be too. You'll have help. You don't need to panic. Health problems or not, this baby will be the most loved, most cared for on the planet.'

He gave her a nudge. 'And who said Tristan didn't have problems? He had killer colic. I compared notes with the guys at work. Our boy could have won the screaming contest every day of the week. Our little guy was hard work.'

Addison's lips tilted upwards a little. 'Is that where you got all the crazy cure-colic ideas from?'

He nodded. 'Yip, and we tried them all. To be honest all the guys really said it wouldn't go away until he started being weaned. But I couldn't tell you that at the time. It's just one of these things that you have to grin and bear.'

She looked surprised. 'You compared notes on our baby?'

'Of course, that's what we guys do.'

The smile disappeared from her face and she put her hand to her stomach. 'And will you do that with this baby?'

She still looked so unsure about everything.

Now he knew what was wrong, he could recognise the look in her eyes. It was fear. And he felt it too.

'Of course I will. I will brag about first smiles, first waves, first tooth and first time they bite me with that tooth.'

He shook his head. 'You've no idea the things that went through my head.'

She wrinkled her nose. 'What are you talking about?'

He ran his fingers through his hair. 'I knew something was wrong. I was worried. Worried that you'd met someone else, worried that you might be sick—'

'You thought I might be sick?'

'I just didn't know. I kept thinking about your sister and...'

She touched his jaw. 'Oh, Caleb.'

'But I totally missed the *she might be pregnant* thing.'

She glanced down at her boobs. 'I was worried you might guess.'

He raised his eyebrows. 'I should have. My observations skills are obviously out of practice.' He frowned for a second as something else crossed his mind. 'What about the alcohol—the cocktails?'

Addison smiled wearily. 'Yeah, that's not been easy. I had to ask that waiter for a nonalcoholic strawberry daiquiri and I've just managed to not drink any of the champagne or wine.'

He opened his mouth in surprise. 'That's what you were doing at the film? I thought the mint thing was strange but never questioned it. I really am slow on the uptake these days, aren't I?'

Addison didn't speak for a few seconds. Then she let out a visible sigh. It was as if all the tension around her neck and shoulders seemed to dissolve. Her whole body just crumpled a little.

For a few moments things had been a bit easier between them. They'd actually been talking. The fault-finding and recriminations had been put aside.

'It was easier when I didn't tell you,' she said.

'What?'

He could see her swallow. 'When I didn't tell you, then all I had to focus on was us—and if we could make it. My head was full of everything. Would I have to move? Where would Tristan go to school? Would you want to see the new baby? How I would cope with the baby. What the impact on Tristan would be if we split.'

He hated hearing those things. He hated that she'd even thought them and he hadn't known. But he could see the bigger picture here. He could see just how truly scared his wife had been.

He closed his hand over hers again. 'And if

you're thinking about all that—then you're not thinking about how our baby will be? If there might be health problems, surgeries. You're not worrying about the future and how they might cope in life. You're not thinking that far ahead and wondering what happens when you and I aren't here any more.'

She briefly closed her eyes. 'Exactly. All the things I'm just terrified to consider.'

Caleb looked out over the bright blue lagoon. He moved his hand back around her shoulders. 'You know, everyone wants their baby to be perfect. Over the years treatment and care for babies and mothers has improved and now they have all these tests. But the thing is, you can't predict everything. Look at the amount of times you hear about things after a kid arrives. Babies can be born with disabilities that aren't picked up on scans. Some babies are perfect right up until delivery—we've all seen the stories in the news about babies getting stuck and having a lack of oxygen. They can have something hidden—like cystic fibrosis. They can develop things. Harry's goddaughter has diabetes. His friends spend their whole life plotting around insulin pumps and eating. The teenage boy at the end of our street had meningitis a few years ago when he started university. What I'm trying to say is there are no guarantees in life. Is it good, or bad, to know what's ahead?'

She clasped her hands in front of her. 'I just don't know.'

His brown eyes were fixed on hers. 'I want you to know something. I want you to know that I'm happy about this baby. I want you to know that hasn't changed. The possibility of having a child that requires surgeries still terrifies me, but this baby? It's ours. It's on its way and I love it already.'

Her lips turned upwards in a grateful smile. 'I do too,' she whispered. 'You've been so good about this. You've been so good to me. I should have told you straight away. I should have spoken to you more. I couldn't even see that I'd started to shut you out. I'm so sorry, honey. I was unfair. I couldn't see beyond my own feelings to think about yours.'

He brushed some loose strands of hair back from her face. 'Thank you for saying that. But we're past that now. We're both past that. We need to look to the future. The future for our family. We need to move forward. We can't keep living in the past.'

The breeze had started to pick up around them and a few more strands of her hair had escaped from her bobble. He stood up and held his hand out towards her. 'Let's get some breakfast. It's probably cold but at least it's something.'

She nodded and put her hand in his. When he pulled her up he pulled her straight into his arms against his chest.

They stood there for a few seconds taking comfort in each other's arms.

Right now, she was the only person that could comfort him, and he was the only person to comfort her. Exactly the way it should be.

It was only morning and she was exhausted again. Probably because she hadn't slept all night.

She had been so determined to just get the words out there the next time she saw him. Keeping it to herself had been too much of a burden. She'd needed to share. She'd needed to be able to talk things through with someone.

Last night he'd been angry with her and she'd felt terrible. She'd reacted badly and then just left because she hadn't been able to deal with the consequences.

This whole time she'd really only been thinking about herself. She hadn't considered Caleb's feelings in any of this. Probably because of how she was feeling.

Now, she realised how unfair she'd been. How well he'd coped with the news she'd just given him. She'd had two weeks to think about things—even though she'd tried not to. But that instant decision—the one she'd made in a heartbeat while on the phone to Dr Mackay—she knew he was right there with her. She should have had faith. She should have believed in her husband.

Now she knew why he'd said he didn't want to expand their family. It wasn't because he didn't care about her. It was exactly the opposite. It was because he did care about her.

He'd had the same worries that she had. Part of it hurt that he hadn't spoken to her—just as she hadn't spoken to him. But in a way, now she understood. She'd struggled to put those thoughts into words just as much as he had. She'd shut him out—even though she hadn't realised she was doing it.

Now, they were ready to face the future together. The weight that had nestled on her shoulders for the last few months had finally came unstuck.

They walked into the kitchen and stopped dead. Tristan was up. He hadn't slept as late as normal and it seemed that he'd helped himself to breakfast.

Tomato ketchup was everywhere. On his face, in his hair and on the table.

Caleb started to laugh and stepped forward.

Tristan's plate was cleared. 'Did you eat all your sausages already?'

He grinned and nodded.

Then Addison noticed something else. She cleared her throat and pointed to the plate where Caleb's breakfast should be. It seemed to have been moved around the plate with one key ingredient missing. 'Did you eat Daddy's sausages too?'

Tristan nodded again, obviously pleased with himself.

'Oh, no,' said Caleb. 'He's over-sausaged. What's the betting he's sick in half an hour?'

She held out her hand to Tristan. 'Let's get you cleaned up while Dad makes me tea.'

A quick shower and change of clothes later Tristan was colouring at the other side of the table.

Caleb set her decaf tea down in front of her along with some toast. He smiled. 'It must be killing you not to drink coffee.'

She shook her head. 'Don't even go there. We're not going to discuss coffee at any point.'

It was odd, watching her husband work about the kitchen in his tuxedo. She was wearing his old clothes with her hair tied up on her head and he still had his suit for the ball on. They must have looked like the oddest couple on the beach.

'Don't you want to get changed?'

'I will. Let's have breakfast first.'

He sat down opposite her. He took a drink of the decaf tea he'd made for himself and grimaced. He was watching her carefully. 'Now I know what's going on, I'd like you to get checked out.'

She put her tea down. 'Why?'

'Because you fainted the other day. You wouldn't let me call a doctor. I should have. I'd like you to get checked out.'

She took a bite of her toast. She had a feeling already that she wasn't going to win this argument. 'I've not had any bleeding, any cramping. It's kind of late for that. I'm past the stage that a miscarriage would normally happen.'

'So what made you faint? Was it your blood pressure?' He shrugged his shoulders. 'I don't know enough about these things. But I'd really like to know there's nothing else to worry about.'

She looked around. 'I'm not sure what kind of maternity services they have around here. I know there's a hospital but I don't know if they have midwives or nurses.'

'We can ask at Reception.' He nodded towards Tristan and mouthed, 'Shall we tell him?'

She was surprised. She hadn't even considered telling Tristan yet, not when she hadn't told her husband. But now there was no reason not to.

She gave a little nod. Caleb turned towards Tristan and picked up a crayon. He started colouring in part of his drawing. 'Hey, Tristan, Mummy and Daddy have got something to tell you.'

Tristan barely acknowledged he'd spoken. His little tongue was poking out and he was concentrating hard on keeping his blue crayon in the lines. He looked up for a second to see what Caleb was doing. 'Make that bit purple, Daddy.'

Caleb gave a nod and picked up a purple crayon. 'How do you feel about babies?'

His eyes widened. 'Jacob at nursery has a baby. So does Lucas and Lily.' He screwed up his nose. 'Lily's baby is a girl.'

Caleb kept going. 'Do they like having little brothers and sisters?'

But Tristan didn't answer the question. Like a typical four-year-old he went off at a tangent. 'My nursery teacher is having a baby. It's hiding in her tummy.'

Caleb glanced at Addison. 'I know someone else who has a baby hiding in their tummy.'

'Is it Mrs Foster? She looks like she has a baby in her tummy.'

Addison let out a giggle. Mrs Foster was their

next-door neighbour and was around eighty years old. She certainly did have a large tummy.

She could tell Caleb was trying not to laugh. 'No. No, it's not Mrs Foster. I don't think she'll have any more babies.' He touched Tristan's arm. 'What about if I told you that Mummy was going to have another baby? Would you like a little brother or sister?'

His head shot up and he stared at Addison open-mouthed. 'We're getting a baby?'

She gave a little nod. 'We are.'

'Can it share my room?'

She could see Caleb trying to be tactful. 'Not right away, but maybe later. When you came home from hospital you had a crib in Mummy and Daddy's room for a few months, then you moved into your own room.'

'The baby will get my room?'

Caleb shook his head. 'No, no. The baby might get the room that's next to yours. Or the one across the hall.'

'Will he be there when we get back home?'

Addison started to laugh. 'What have you done? I think we'll get these questions for the next six months.' She leaned forward and grasped Tristan's hand. 'Do you want to come and feel my tummy? The baby is in there right now but it's still quite small.' She tried to think in kids' terms. 'It will come after Halloween and before Christmas.'

Tristan jumped down from the chair and ran around the table, putting his hand on her stomach. 'My nursery teacher's tummy is much bigger than that. Can we visit the fish again today?'

And that was that.

He was four. His attention span had moved on to the next thing. She was relieved that he seemed happy. There was no need to tell him anything else. There was plenty of time for that.

Caleb swept him up into his arms. 'How about we go and have a look at some of the fishes under the water bungalow?'

'Yeah, Daddy!'

They came back fifteen minutes later when she'd finally showered and changed out of Caleb's T-shirt and into a pale blue dress. Caleb stripped off his tuxedo and jumped in the shower straight after her. He was ready ten minutes later and picked up Tristan with one hand and held out his other towards her. 'Ready?'

Was she? She put her bag over her shoulder. 'Yes. Let's go.'

The staff at Reception were well trained. It only took one phone call to arrange for her to see one of the local doctors at the hospital. They even arranged transport for them.

Her stomach churned nervously. She was sure

she was fine. She was sure. So why was she so nervous?

Caleb reached forward and took her hand again. Tristan was playing with his wrestlers. He hadn't even asked any questions about where they were.

'Addison, before you go in, I want you to know something.'

'What?' She couldn't stop the anxiety in her voice.

His brown eyes met hers. 'I want you to know that I love you. I want you to know that I'm with you every step of the way. No matter what news we get today, or in the future, I'm going to be right by your side. I'm sorry it's taken me this long to get my priorities in order. I'm sorry that I didn't tell you the truth about being worried.' He pressed his hand to his heart. 'I'm happy about this baby. I really am. Yes, I'm still worried and I'll probably ask Dr Mackay a hundred questions when we get back. But whatever happens was meant to be. I believe that. Ten years ago I met the woman of my dreams. And she still blows me away every single day.'

A tear slid down her cheek.

'I only want a life with you. I can't begin to imagine life without you. If our next baby is a night-time screamer then I'm on duty. I'm on duty to do whatever you want.' He reached into his pocket and pulled out a crumpled piece of paper. 'I wrote this last night when I was sitting on the beach. I have to tell you it was the easiest thing I've ever done.'

She took the paper with a trembling hand and unfolded it. There, in Caleb's characteristic scrawling writing—with a few words scored out here and there—was the finest thing she'd ever seen.

*Connor and Shaw Associates are looking for a dynamic and motivated individual to become the third partner within their firm...*

'I'll get the advert posted as soon as we get home.' He pulled a receipt out of his other pocket. 'I've also written an advert for the three assistants. It's time for me to prioritise. And that's you, Addison. It's always been you. I guess I just got lost a little along the way.'

She gave a nod. 'I'll phone your secretary and put all our appointments in your schedule. I love you, Caleb. I've always loved you, even when I tried to convince myself that I didn't. I don't want to do this alone. I want to do this with you. I want to know that if we get told something scary that we can cope and be strong. I promise I'll listen to whatever you have to say.'

Caleb lifted her hand and placed it on his chest. 'I need you, Addison. I need you every single day. I can't be *me*, without *you*. Don't doubt for a second how much I love you.'

They were the words she'd wanted to hear for so long. It was the reassurance that he would make time for her, Tristan and this new baby. It was relief that if she needed to talk, if she needed to cry, she could do it with the person who was the most important to her. If she was scared, she could tell him. If she needed help, she could tell him. If she just wanted him to hold her hand, he would be there.

He reached up with a thumb and brushed her tear away. 'Don't cry, honey. Let's celebrate our baby,' he whispered.

'Mrs Connor?' The voice startled them. A doctor in a white coat was standing in the corridor. He held out his hand when she nodded. 'I'm Dr Akana. Please come this way.'

Caleb squeezed her hand before she stood. 'You're the strongest woman I know. Whatever happens, it happens to us.'

He was sincere. He meant every word and even though she was terrified it made her heart sing.

The doctor led them along to a consulting room. Tristan immediately sat in a corner playing with his wrestlers.

The doctor invited her to sit down and checked her file. 'Mrs Connor, I understand that you're pregnant and had a fall a few days ago?'

She gave a nod.

He moved around the desk and sat next to her. 'If you don't mind, I'll ask some questions and examine you.'

'That's fine.'

He was thorough, checking her obstetric history, the story of her fall, asking about any pain, cramping or bleeding, then checking her blood pressure and urine.

She paused for a second. 'I had some…news.'

He looked up from his notes. She could almost see him choosing his words carefully. 'Okay, then, what kind of news?'

She bit her lip. 'My nuchal screening test put me at high risk.'

He glanced at the dates on her chart. 'I take it you found out just before you came on holiday?'

She nodded.

'And you didn't decide on any more testing?'

She shook her head firmly.

He gave her a reassuring smile. 'I want to be clear. Everything is looking fine. The purpose of today is to just check you and the baby are okay—I won't be able to tell you any more about your nuchal screening. I'll leave that for your obstetrician back home. Are you okay with that?'

She glanced at Caleb and gave a nod.

'Would you like to hop up on the trolley and I'll have a feel of your tummy and check for a heartbeat?'

She felt a little surge of panic. Instinct wanted her to run from the room but that was just silly. Caleb appeared beside her, putting his arm around her and almost carrying her along and over to the trolley.

She sat down and swung her legs around, lifting her dress to reveal her slightly swollen tummy. The doctor washed and warmed his hands before touching her. He was quick. 'Everything feels right for your dates. No pain anywhere that I'm touching?'

She shook her head. He pulled the ultrasound machine over. 'Just a little gel on your tummy,' he said as he opened the tube and turned the machine on.

She couldn't breathe. Caleb must have seen the panic on her face as he moved around to the other side of the trolley and held her hand.

Dr Akana positioned the probe and swept it over her abdomen. He took a quick look at the screen. 'I won't be able to tell you anything else about being high risk. This scan is just to check baby is thriving. Have you booked in for a detailed scan at twenty weeks?'

'The appointment should be waiting when I go back.'

He nodded. 'That's good.' He pointed at the screen. 'Here we are, baby is looking good. Here's the skull, the spine, this is the femur—the thigh bone and this little flicker is the heartbeat.'

She let out her breath as Caleb squeezed her hand again. His eyes were fixed on the screen and he had a wide smile on his face. 'Hey, Tristan,' he said. 'Come over here and have a look at your little brother or sister.'

Tristan's head shot up and he walked over, staring at the screen.

Dr Akana pointed out the parts of the baby to him just as baby started kicking. Tristan let out a squeal. 'Look at that! He wants to play football.'

'*He* might be a she,' said Addison quickly. 'We don't know yet.'

Caleb's eyes hadn't moved from the screen. 'Would it be possible to get a printout?' He seemed transfixed.

Instantly she felt guilty. Last time around he'd come to every appointment with her. He'd been more nervous than her when it had come to the first scan. This time she'd gone alone—

and cheated him out of his first chance to see their child.

Dr Akana nodded and pressed a button before lifting the probe and wiping her stomach clean. He tore the picture from the machine and handed it to Caleb before helping Addison down from the trolley.

'Everything looks fine, Mrs Connor. I think your earlier thoughts about not eating and drinking enough could be true. Your urine is clear, your blood pressure fine and I can't see anything else to worry about for now.'

The relief was instant. 'Thank you,' she said quickly.

He stood up to shake her hand. 'If you have any other concerns, or you feel unwell, you can come back and see me any time.'

Five minutes later they were outside and in the car heading back to the resort.

Addison leaned against her husband as he wrapped his arms around her. It was the first time in the last few years she'd felt happy and secure. The worries were still there, but this time they were shared. This time, they weren't just hers.

They were in this together. They wouldn't repeat their past mistakes. They'd learned and they'd grown together as a couple—as a family. If she was scared, or unsure, or felt the slightest bit numb, this time she would talk to her husband. She wouldn't think there was something wrong with her. She wouldn't think she was failing. She'd realise that it was probably hormonal—probably outside her control—and just try to work through it with the support of the man that loved her.

'What do you want to do tonight?' he asked.

She smiled and glanced at Tristan, who looked up at her with his big eyes. She knew exactly how to answer this question.

She turned her head to plant a kiss on Caleb's lips. 'We're in Bora Bora. What else? I want to lie in our big bed in the water bungalow and watch the fish with my two favourite men in the world.'

He nodded. 'Your wish is my command.'

And it was.

# EPILOGUE

'Push, honey, push.'

It was official. Caleb felt one hundred per cent useless.

'Almost there,' said the midwife reassuringly as she looked up from her position at the bottom of the bed.

He was at the top end, Addison leaning back against him, exhausted and panting.

The twenty-week scan hadn't shown any clear abnormalities. The nuchal measurement was still slightly enlarged and they'd accepted it was a wait-and-see situation.

This morning Addison had felt tired and Caleb had volunteered to take Tristan out to the park for a while.

One hour later she'd been in hard labour. Caleb's mobile had rung merrily in the kitchen when she'd tried to phone him and Reuben had practically broken every rule of the road getting her to the hospital before screeching back to the park to find Caleb.

'Don't tell me to push. You push.'

He took a deep breath. He needed to be strong for his beautiful wife, even though he was terrified for her. She gripped his hand again as another contraction hit and he watched the colour drain out of his fingers, then they changed to an attractive shade of blue.

Reuben and Lara were sitting outside with Tristan. All waiting for baby news. When they'd got back from Bora Bora his best friend was engaged to his nanny. Reuben had wanted to get married as soon as possible, but since Lara wanted Addison to be her witness they'd decided to wait until after the baby was here.

Now, they were all waiting.

'Here comes the head,' shouted the midwife with a big smile on her face.

Addison let out a scream. 'Aargh…'

Caleb held his breath. This was it. This was the moment they'd both been waiting for.

'Head's out, pant now, Addison,' said the midwife.

Caleb's throat was bone dry. He wanted to be down at the bottom of the bed, he wanted to watch his child come into the world but Addison needed him here.

The midwife changed her position. 'Okay,

folks, get ready for the next contraction and baby will be here.'

He'd be lucky if he could ever use his hands again. But he didn't really care. Anything was worth it. His family was worth it.

Addison gritted her teeth. 'Come on,' she shouted as her face turned redder and redder.

Ten seconds later baby was out and flipped up onto her chest.

The paediatrician was here and waiting. The neonatal unit had a bed ready if needed.

Addison's hand reached up, touching her baby's back and cradling baby towards her. Caleb bent forward for a better look. He hadn't heard any noise yet.

Baby was looking right at him, unblinking with a scowl on its face. As he watched there was a little shudder as air was sucked in and baby's colour started to pink up.

He'd never seen anything so beautiful.

He glanced downwards. They'd decided not to find out what they were having this time. 'Hey.' He touched Addison's cheek. 'Tristan will be mad. We've got a daughter.'

'A daughter?' She was still catching her breath. Her eyes filled up with tears. 'A daughter. We've got a daughter.'

Caleb was still looking at his daughter's scowling face and watching her little chest rise and fall when the paediatrician tapped his shoulders. The little girl that would probably break his heart a million times over and give him a nervous breakdown. He couldn't wait.

'Breathing seems fine. But do you mind if I check her over?'

The midwife looked up. 'Dad? Do you want to cut the cord?'

He nodded and walked to the bottom of the bed, taking the scissors with slightly shaking hands. He cut between the clamps and watched as the paediatrician carried his daughter over to the crib with the heat lamp for a few minutes.

Addison started to shake a little. So he walked back and put his arm around her shoulders. 'I hate to break it to you,' he said, 'but even though her eyes are blue, they're on the dark side. I think she's going to take after her dad.'

'Just as long as she doesn't inherit your talent for snoring.' Addison was smiling. She looked exhausted. The labour had been quick and two weeks early, catching them all a little by surprise.

The paediatrician was listening to their daughter's chest. 'Sophie?' Caleb asked.

She nodded, her smile getting broader by the second. 'Yes, definitely Sophie.'

The second midwife was over next to the paediatrician, writing down a few notes, then wiping baby's face and body.

The paediatrician wrapped her blanket loosely around her and carried her back. 'Well, she might be two weeks early but at seven pounds fifteen ounces you might be glad of that.' He gave them a reassuring nod as he handed her back. 'Breathing and observations are fine, heart and lungs clear and—' he met both their gazes '—no sign of anything else.'

'Really?' Addison's question was almost a whisper.

The paediatrician gave a clear reply. 'Really.'

Her breath came out in a whoosh.

'Do you want five minutes?' asked the midwife. She understood. She understood completely.

'Please,' said Caleb.

The midwife handed over the buzzer. 'I'm right outside.'

The two midwives and paediatrician filed out.

Caleb moved behind Addison again, letting her lean back against him with their daughter back on her chest.

'Welcome to the world, Sophie.' He moved his hand over Addison's and intertwined his fingers with hers.

'Thank you, Caleb,' Addison whispered.

'What are you thanking me for? You're the one that's done all the hard work.'

She shook her head. 'Thank you for the last six months. Thank you for keeping your promises.'

He reached up and touched her cheek. 'Love you, Addison Connor. Nothing else is more important than you and our family.'

He planted a kiss on her lips. 'I've never been happier.'

'Me either.'

And together they watched their little daughter give a little squirm, then a little cry. Addison smiled. 'There could be trouble ahead.'

'Can't wait.'

Then he kissed her again and went outside to introduce their son and friends to the latest member of the Connor family.

\* \* \* \* \*

*Don't miss the first book in*
*Scarlet Wilson's*
TYCOONS IN A MILLION *duet*
*HOLIDAY WITH THE MILLIONAIRE*
*Available now!*

*Prince Alexandros Sanchos is marrying out of
obligation—for custom and for duty.
But how will he react when his royal bride
is determined to capture his heart?*

*Read on for a sneak preview of
WEDDED FOR HIS ROYAL DUTY,
the second book in* Susan Meier's *duet
THE PRINCES OF XAVIERA.*

Eva stared into his eyes, a million confusing truths racing
through her brain. This was the unspoken reality of what
happened to people with destinies. It was all there in his
eyes. People with destinies rarely got what they wanted.
Duty and responsibility came first.

Would she throw it all away for one night with a man
she longed for? The first man she'd ever really wanted?

She swallowed. She'd thought the answer would be
easy. Instead, she stood frozen. How could she decide
without a kiss? Without a touch?

Her lips tingled at the thought of another kiss. Her
entire body exploded at the thought of more of his touch.
Something must have changed in her expression because
he pulled back. "No. I can't be the person who steals your
destiny from you."

Her eyes clung to his. "There is one way."

His eyebrows rose.

"I know I told you I wouldn't force you to stay
married…but what if we wanted to?"

"Stay married?"

She nodded.

He squeezed his eyes shut. "You have known me four weeks. I can't ask for a life commitment after four weeks."

"But you were willing to marry a princess you didn't know."

"And now I know her and now I know she deserves more. Real love. Trust. A man who doesn't have walls."

He turned her in the direction of her room. "Go, before I can't be noble anymore."

*Don't miss*
***WEDDED FOR HIS ROYAL DUTY***
*by Susan Meier,*
*available July 2016 wherever*
*Harlequin® Romance books and ebooks are sold.*

www.Harlequin.com

# Reading Has Its Rewards

## Earn **FREE BOOKS!**

Register at **Harlequin My Rewards** and submit your Harlequin purchases from wherever you shop to earn points for free books and other exclusive rewards.

Plus submit your purchases from now till May 30th for a chance to win a $500 Visa Card*.

## Visit **HarlequinMyRewards.com** today

MYR16R1